Everlong

Praise for Hailey Edward's
Everlong

"Everlong by Hailey Edwards is a blend of paranormal romance and fantasy guaranteed to enchant readers of both genres. ...Adventure, fascinating characters, exotic places and sensual romance combine to provide an entertaining read."

~ *Books and Blurbs*

"Everlong was a fabulous paranormal/fantasy romance. ...This story has everything you could possible wish for: a great plot, fantastic characters, mystery, intrigue, romance, and a nice twist to the ending. ...If you are looking for a great paranormal/fantasy romance that is easy to read and continuously flows from beginning to end, then Everlong is definitely the book for you."

~ *Manic Readers*

"...I can't begin to tell you how pleased I am with Everlong by Hailey Edwards. It's a story about forgiveness, breaking out of your shell, and allowing yourself to love someone with all your heart. I sincerely hope there will be more stories in this world. ...Very well done, Hailey!"

~ *Bitten by Books*

"Whew! Everlong should come with a three hankie warning on it! ...While this story not only satisfied this reviewer's inner romantic side, it also throws in a healthy dose of paranormal with some absolutely delicious demons. ...Ms. Edwards not only balanced the romance in this book with the sci-fi genre, she did a superb job of it. The creativeness of this author amazed me. ...Kudos to Ms. Edwards for writing such an intricate tale of love."

~ *Dark Diva Reviews*

"If you enjoy fantasy and hunky winged-demons — then this is the book for you."

~ *Anna's Book Blog*

Everlong

Hailey Edwards

SAMHAIN
PUBLISHING

Samhain Publishing, Ltd.
577 Mulberry Street, Suite 1520
Macon, GA 31201
www.samhainpublishing.com

Everlong
Copyright © 2011 by Hailey Edwards
Print ISBN: 978-1-60928-003-1
Digital ISBN: 978-1-60504-953-3

Editing by Sasha Knight
Cover by Tuesday Dube

First Samhain Publishing, Ltd. electronic publication: March 2010
First Samhain Publishing, Ltd. print publication: January 2011

Dedication

To Michael and Chickaboo. You two (almost) never complain when dinner is late, burned or cold so I can finish writing down an idea.

To Dad. Your support and encouragement mean so much to me. Mom, I promise one day to write a book where things are blown up just for you.

To Cait, my right-hand woman, and my dear friend, Melanie.

Chapter One

Realm of Askara, City of Rihos

Impact jarred my bones as one swift kick from Emma introduced my back to the floor of the courtyard. My head thumped dully against the ground, snapping together teeth over tongue and filling my mouth with a fresh burst of coppery liquid.

Through the dust stirred up by our sparring, her brows knit together over serious azure eyes.

We weren't blood related, but she was my sister in all the ways that mattered.

"You win." Shooting pain stabbed my lungs on each shallow inhale. "I think something's broken." I curbed the whine from my voice before she heard it too.

"Maddie, this is the third time this week." The training stick fell from her hands to land with a hollow thud.

I watched the stick roll just out of her reach and breathed easier.

She dropped to the hard ground beside me and dug her knees into my tender side. Another whimper forced its way out over my bruised lips. "Stop whining." Emma inched closer. "It's not that bad. The bone didn't even break the skin this time. Just hold still for a minute."

Her brows gathered again as she walked her fingers across my chest, tracing the lines of each rib from base to tip. Midway down my sternum, I hissed, "That's the one."

She acted like she hadn't heard and tapped the sore spot with her pointed fingernail. "You mean this one?" *Tap.* "This rib right here?" *Tap. Tap.*

Pain flared bright red behind my eyes. "Poke me with your finger one more time and I swear to Zaniah, I will rip it from your hand."

One side of her mouth quirked upward in a wry smile. "If you had the nerve to back that up, I might be scared." Her gaze raked me from head to toe. "But you don't." Soft curls bounced around her face. "You're pathetic. The first female born of the two demon houses and you're weaker than a kitten."

The insult was so unexpected, so brutal, I couldn't think past it. I didn't register the decision my brain made to punch Emma, so I'm not sure which of us was more surprised to find my fist planted in her face. Cartilage crunched under my knuckles and blood ran from her nose like a sieve. My mouth opened on a gasp.

"If you say you're sorry," she growled, "I'll thread your rib through your lung for you. It's about time you started sticking up for yourself."

I bared my own bloodstained teeth in a grin and rolled the shoulder she'd dislocated earlier. "I was just going to ask if you could bleed someplace else. You're drenching me."

Her pale pink lips were painted red and swollen, much the same as mine. She spat on the ground, then dropped into a sprawl across the patch of dirt beside me and took my hand in hers.

Her fingers squeezed. Mine squeezed back, our injuries already forgiven and forgotten. Emma's minor wounds would mend within the hour, mine knitted together even now. We knew from experience the bones she'd broken in me would heal after a solid night's rest. We had no cause to hold on to insults or anger.

"So." She cleared her throat. "Tomorrow is our big day. Have you given any thought to the color you'll choose for us?"

I willed the vibrant blue sky overhead to hold my attention. I didn't want to think about tomorrow while we had borrowed time left today, but the thoughts tumbled out one after another.

My ascension was the final step in claiming my title as an Askaran heiress, not that I wanted it or even needed the confirmation as second in line for the throne. I would never rule Askara. That unpleasant task fell to my elder sister, Nesvia. Still, the kingdom expected a spectacle and Mother did enjoy putting on a show.

"Maddie?" Her elbow jabbed my side.

I winced. "I chose lavender."

Her fingers traced lazy circles, loops and swirls across her cheeks and pert nose. "My favorite color."

"Yes," I said. "It is."

For all the difference it would make. By this time tomorrow, ritualistic tattoos would cover our bodies. Mine would denote my lineage. Hers would be an ornate branding to identify her owner, the royal house of Askara.

Emma tensed and dug her fingernails into my palm seconds before a long, dark shadow cast across my face. Squinting into the sun, I glanced up and caught a hint of tailored black velvet breeches adorned with the silver threads symbolic of First Court consorts. The pants were topped with a similar dark shirt and matching vest. The heavy embroidery indicated how high up the social ladder my stepfather had managed to climb.

"Lord Archer."

I didn't miss his flicker of interest when his gaze roved over the blood and sweat slicking my skin. I'd seen the same expression too many times to mistake its cause.

"Princess Madelyn."

Formality hardened the tone he used when calling on business rather than pleasure. Emma's grip loosened. He hadn't come for us. Not this time at least.

I offered thanks to the divine goddess that Askaran nobles prized virginity. I could not be touched until after my ascendancy, and as my chosen handmaiden, neither could Emma. But our meager protection's expiration date was fast approaching, as evidenced by his arrival.

"Queen Eliya wishes me to remind you that your ascendancy ceremony is tomorrow, and that you are to be prepared for her personal inspection no less than one hour prior to its commencement."

Archer nudged Emma's shoulder with the toe of his dress shoe, then stomped the ground below her ear as if he would enjoy crushing her face beneath his heel.

Assured of her attention, he addressed her. "Emmaline, you will prepare your ward to the queen's exact specifications. Tomorrow is a very important day for the royal line." He glanced between us. "Even the bastards."

Emma pushed from the ground to her feet and leaned down to offer me a grimy but much-needed hand up. "Careful." She lifted me slowly until my feet bore my own weight. Halflings were remarkably stronger than either their demon or human parentage, and she was no exception.

He appraised me a second time. His icy fingers brushed a trail from the waistband of my bloused white pants, across my bare midriff and upwards until they touched the fabric ending just below my breasts. Loathing caused me to shiver beneath his touch.

Slapping away his hand only elicited another spark of sickening interest. He lifted the hand he'd caressed me with and inhaled the tips of his fingers. My lips curled with disgust.

"You cannot find my stench appealing." Blood mixed with dirt to crust my palms and knees. Salt stung my eyes and dusted my skin as sweat dried.

His eyes gleamed brighter. "You have no idea." His ensuing laughter smacked of his superiority, as if he knew something I had yet to guess. Any secrets he held could only be as vile as I found him, and I wished them to stay locked in his conscious rather than burdening mine.

"What happened to her?" he asked Emma, the unspoken *without my permission* clear behind his words.

"It was an accident while sparring, Father," she said. "It's nothing serious. This type of break never takes more than a few hours to heal."

"I'm well aware of her regenerative capabilities." The smile he turned my way made gooseflesh ripple across my chilled skin. "I never dreamed she would have such an unexpected genetic quirk. That marvelous ability to heal shouldn't be wasted." His lips pursed. "I suppose we'll simply have to continue testing her limits."

"Is that what you call it?" Emma snapped. "Testing her limits?" She held her hands outstretched for us to see. "You use *my* hands to break her. It's *my* hands covered in her blood and *my* shoulder she cries on while her bones mend."

His eyes hardened. "You aren't suggesting I enjoy what has to be done to Madelyn?"

"Oh no, Father. That would make you a monster."

The crack of flesh meeting flesh resounded in the enclosed yard.

My shoulders bunched, bracing for an impact that didn't come. Glancing up, I watched Archer's struggle for composure in the tense lines of his shoulders and the sweat dampening his brow. Emma's scowling face bore the imprint of her father's hand.

"Never take it upon yourself to hurt Madelyn this way again." His gaze swept the scuffed-up earth beneath our feet and passed over the training stick a few yards away. "She's too weak to be properly trained. It's a waste of your time and talent."

"And he wouldn't find me half as amusing if I could defend myself." Shaking my head, I tried to clear away the rebellious thoughts streaming through my mind.

"Bite your tongue, girl."

I almost told him I already had. I'd awakened today transformed with an odd sense of purpose. I wanted to train, was ready to fight, ready for something. It was the only reason Emma agreed to the quick match even knowing Archer was on his way. She had known I needed to dull the edge of whatever consumed me.

"Maddie's fast. With more training she could become a valued—"

Archer's mirthless laughter cut off her retort. "Her greatest value lies in breathing."

One hand caught the end of my wheat blonde braid, snatching my head back as he used my hair like a rope to drag me against him. Hair ripped free of my scalp, making my eyes water as his other hand cinched around my rib cage and squeezed until the tears overflowed onto my cheeks.

I couldn't breathe through the acute agony of his hold as

each caress dug his fingers deeper into bruised and aching flesh. I sank a sharp elbow into his soft gut, but he only pulled harder, rewarding pain with pain.

"So long as her heart beats, her mother's throne is secure." The arm banding me tightened as he leaned in, brushing my cheek with his nose before drawing my scent into his lungs. "The queen requires an heir to keep her title." He shrugged. "In the unfortunate event something happened to her elder sister, Madelyn would enable Eliya to keep her crown. The royal line must be kept established...and fertile." He hummed gruffly in my ear then shoved me away from him.

Humiliation warmed my cheeks as hatred filled my heart for the man who was father to me by name, but sire to Emma by blood. For a tense moment, I thought he might come at me again, but he didn't get the chance.

"My lord Archer," an Evanti slave called from across the courtyard. He broke away from his peers while jogging steadily in our direction. The familiar black-skinned courier wore only a thin scrap of leather around his hips and the great, carmine wings that marked his breed. He advanced until he stood squarely between Archer and me.

A move not lost on my stepfather.

"Harper," Emma whispered just loud enough for him to hear. "Don't do anything foolish."

Harper's wings twitched in agitation and tucked closer against his bare back before he addressed Archer.

"Your presence is required at First Court."

"Is it now?" Archer tilted his head, catching my eye over the curve of Harper's shoulder. He reached just behind Harper's back and tugged the thick wrist of one wing. "I wonder, slave. Will Madelyn's virtue be found intact on the morrow? Or will we discover she's been lying with her guardian?" His thumb stroked the thin, filmy skin of Harper's wing. "Unfortunately, sometimes the apple does not fall far from the tree. Her mother suffered a similar taste for darker flesh."

Fear tightened my gut. "Harper has nothing to do with this. Release him, now."

I didn't dare to breathe until Archer's hand dropped. This time he left the silky skin intact, and I could have thanked him for it.

"Harper, is it? How quaint, you've named him." He smiled as if amused. "You're really not so different from your mother. She would barter her soul to keep her seat upon the throne." He stroked a finger down Harper's forearm. "And I know the price of your soul as well."

I met Archer's level stare with disinterest, unwilling to let him see how his dawning comprehension terrified me.

Then he spoke to Harper. "You do realize how far beneath her you are, don't you? Her bloodlines alone will harm her chances of finding a proper consort. Her affection for you only lessens her prospects," he said with false sincerity. "Even her Evanti father had some status within your race. What could you possibly think you have to offer her? She's Askaran royalty and you're just...her pet."

"I am in her service, my lord, nothing more." Harper stood silent and unmoving.

Archer stared a moment longer, seeming to decide something before losing interest and wiping his fingers across his thigh. He turned on his well-tailored heels and stalked towards the arched metal gate leading through the heavy stone wall of the summer castle and out into the desert sands of Rihos.

Once Archer reached the gatekeeper and boarded his transport, Harper followed in steady, measured strides. He glanced over his shoulder and pointed once towards the entrance to the grand hall. Beside me, Emma nodded her agreement.

I held my breath as his wings outstretched and thrust downward to launch him into the sky. He would follow Archer to the border before returning home to me. If his flight took longer than the few hours necessary to make the round trip, I never said a word. His face shined with joy as he made the leap skyward, making me smile for long minutes after he became a distant dot on my horizon.

Chapter Two

I jerked upright in bed as a scream ripped from my throat. I slapped a hand over my mouth while my body fought to flush the surge of adrenaline making my limbs tingle and muscles tighten. My heart pounded a deafening cadence in my ears as the remnants of my dream faded from memory.

Like all females of my line, I was night blind. Nothing permeated the absolute darkness surrounding me. My nighttime curfew had never been enforced since I didn't dare leave my room after dark. Not all Evanti were as forgiving of my parentage as Harper, and their flawless night vision wouldn't miss my bumbling attempts to find my way through the gloom.

Only the tangle of silken sheets around my ankles and the give of soft mattress beneath my palms assured me I was in my room and safe. Falling back into the pile of pillows littering my bed, I rested my palm across my chest. My heart punched urgently beneath my hand.

Was my nightmare the same night after night or something new? I didn't know. I never remembered more than the sound of my own screams and the shattering sense of loss I felt upon waking.

The groan of metal twisting drew my attention in the direction I knew the door to be. Heavy wood creaked on worn hinges, spilling light into my room and illuminating the stark outline of my guest before the tumblers clicked back into place, locking him inside with me.

I heard a sharp, rasping sound seconds before the room began to glow.

"Bad dream?" Harper asked around a tongue still thick with sleep.

"No, at least, I don't think so."

I heard him move closer. The dim light cast from his oil lamp focused my eyes. The flame flickered and danced while painting fanciful reflections on the walls and floor. "I think tomorrow..." I glanced over at him. "I'm afraid."

He didn't waste words on placations neither of us would believe. "Move over." His velvety whisper tickled my ears as the mattress dipped and he joined me on the bed. "Sit up."

I arched a brow at him, watching his angular face soften with amusement.

His black eyes caught the light and shined with warmth while his full lips broke into a crooked grin. Then he softened his command. "Please."

"You really shouldn't have come." He reached for me, but I batted away his hands. "You know what will happen if you're caught in here after dark." Thick scar tissue crisscrossed his back. Vivid reminders of the price he had already paid.

"Yes, Zaniah forbid the wolf bed down with his sheep." His derisive snort brought a faint curve to my lips. "I was bred to serve you. I'm only doing what I was born to do." His finger traced the slope of my nose. "Lucky for us both I enjoy my work."

"Harper..." Archer had been right. I would have sold my soul to buy his freedom. What good were his wings if he would never be free to use them?

"Shh." He pressed that same rough finger to my lips. "I'm yours, lady, and I will never leave your side." He glanced around, seeming to survey not just the room, but the entire kingdom beyond the castle walls. "I could never leave you in this place." Then his bright white teeth flashed. "And don't think for a moment I would remain if not for you, and Emma."

I playfully slapped his chest, content to pretend he, at least, had other options. Even if a haven existed, I doubted an Askaran royal would be welcomed there. Most likely I would be turned away, if not worse.

I'd heard whispers of an Evanti uprising. All of Rihos buzzed with the news of slaves gone missing under the cover of night and stores of food and supplies being raided. I was likely the only member of the nobility hoping, praying, that the rumors were true and wishing my slaves would vanish next.

Harper captured my hand where it still rested against his chest and pulled me into a sitting position. I flinched as pain seized my upper back.

"You don't have to do this every time, you know." I could only imagine how I appeared to him. Puny and pale, wingless and weak, nothing worthy of the devotion he gave me so freely.

"You might as well cooperate. I won't leave while you're in pain." He tugged the hem of my nightgown up around my hips and exposed the pale coral of my silken undergarments.

"Stubborn male," I accused.

Harper laughed, the sound as dark as the night surrounding us. "I'm not the stubborn one." He tugged the sweat-dampened nightgown over my head to land softly on the stones. "Now, roll over."

I growled at him, but the sound lacked any real heat. In truth, I needed the relief he offered me.

Flopping onto my stomach, I pushed my face into my

buckwheat pillow. The hulls shifted and sifted around as they conformed to my new position. "Fine," I groused. "Just don't look, all right?" As if he hadn't seen my back bared a thousand times since childhood. "I hate for you to see me this way."

Wearing nothing but the same scrap of leather tied around his narrow hips, Harper straddled my legs and leaned over me, kneading away the aches sandwiching my spine.

"Oh, Maddie." Sadness laced his voice.

The sound of his pity grated in my ears. I pushed up, but he forced me down with a gentle hand to the small of my back.

"I know they're hideous," I snapped, closer to tears than I cared to admit. "I told you not to look."

"They" I called them, making it easier to forget *they* were a part of *me*.

His fingers dug into the skin of my lower back still pinned beneath his palm. "You're beautiful." His warm breath fanned my skin. I shivered as he kissed the bony knuckles protruding behind my shoulder blades. "And you can have the use of my wings whenever you need them."

His chest lowered to press against my back, and his leathery wings enfolded us like a living blanket. His bare skin warmed me. His chin rested on my shoulder, placing us cheek to cheek as his fingers interlaced with mine and tightened.

The steady beat of his heart soothed me, guiding my own to rest.

Morning had almost passed and noon approached in steady increments tapped out by my numb fingers against my slick thigh. Mother would arrive at any moment.

I heard the yawn of my bedroom door opening and turned too quickly, pitching forward on unsteady legs and cinching my fingers around the gilded frame of my oval mirror. Its spindly stand creaked against my added weight, but I couldn't feel my hands to make them release the heavy wood. I couldn't feel...anything.

A topical anesthetic saturated my skin, making it glisten in the morning light streaming in from the stained-glass windows. The herbal drink Emma had given me upon waking made my mind run in wider, looser circles.

"How are you holding up?" Emma padded softly into the room wearing a white silk robe tied with a sash around her waist. Her feet were as bare as my body. A bun tamed her riotous curls, pulling her eyes up towards her hairline and lending them an exotic slant.

"Goomph." Dry and thick, my tongue rolled the word around, failing to get it out on the first try. "Good, I'm...good." As well as could be expected, all things considered.

"Are you ready?" Her words were mumbled around the thumbnail caught between her teeth.

"It won't hurt," I slurred. "Harper promised it wouldn't hurt."

His desperation to make good on that promise had resulted in an extra hour, an extra application of the thick, gelatinous goo used to numb the topmost layers of my skin.

Through the haze fogging my mind, I looked again at the crisp, white silk robe Emma wore. It should have been slicked to her skin instead of floating just above it. Dread pooled low in my belly. "Why haven't you been prepared?"

She wouldn't look at me. "As a testament of my devotion to you, I'm to go through the ritual without aid." Her voice hardened. "Father insisted."

The bottom dropped out of my queasy stomach. "No, you can't go through with this."

"I have no choice." Her chin jerked up another notch. "I will prove he cannot break me."

"You don't have to prove anything. You have me, *vinda larsh*, and I won't allow you to suffer needlessly."

"No, *vinda koosh*, you are the one who has me. I've been in your service since the day you were born." She laughed bitterly. Then her attention settled where I grasped the mirror's frame. "What's that in your hand?"

I glanced down, having forgotten I still held a missive now pasted to my skin. "This arrived shortly after you left." I passed over the limp document bearing the royal consort's black wax seal. "I assume to give me time to come to terms with the contents before facing you. Archer must have known you would try and talk me out of it."

Emma scanned the document with a downward sweep of her eyes. "Zaniah be merciful," she whispered. "You can't mean to go through with this."

"If I don't, then you and Harper will be taken." I faked interest in my ink-smudged fingertips. "Archer assured me of that."

The paper edges tore where her fingers punched through parchment. "He can't do this." She crushed the note in her hand. "He won't force this on you, you can't allow it." She stared at the paper like she would a serpent poised to strike before hurling it across the room.

"If I don't agree," I said, "then he will take Harper to the outlands and leave him there to work the silver mines until he dies. Can you imagine what that would do to him? Being trapped underground and never seeing the sky? Never using his wings?"

Her jaw twitched. I could almost hear the grinding of her molars, but she let me speak.

"And you? Sold into service as a courtesan? You are his daughter and he would offer you to the First Court vultures or the highest bidder." I regained my balance and stared her down. "He will not have either of you. Not if I can stop him."

She grabbed my shoulders and shook with enough force to rock me back on my heels. "Did you not see the price? He wants you to *claim* him. An ascendant has first choice of any male the night of her ascendancy. If you choose him, the queen will have to abide by your decision." Her hands dropped. "We aren't worth it. Nothing is worth enduring that."

I cupped her face with my hands, smoothing my thumbs over her cheeks and down her neck. Little of her skin was exposed above the silk of her robe, but I hoped everywhere I touched would absorb the anesthetic gel coating mine.

"You are my sister, and Harper..." I thought of those coarse ridges marring his once satin skin. "I can name each whip's mark and what he did to earn every lash. He's paid enough for our friendship."

"It doesn't matter—"

I silenced Emma by holding up my hand. "If I accept Archer tonight, he will bring a notary and transfer your indentures to me." The prospect almost made me giddy. I blamed the drink for making everything seem more agreeable. "You will both belong to me. No one could ever take either of you away. We'll have to stay here in Rihos, but—"

"And then what? You will have *bedded* him. Do you honestly think he'll stop after one night? He will never be satisfied. How can you sell yourself so cheaply? Where is your pride?"

"Pride isn't everything. Not to me."

"My pride is all I have." Her pale cheeks flushed pink. "You are the princess. I am the handmaiden who is one step from being a First Court whore."

Tears pricked my eyes, so I stared at the ceiling, counting gilded tiles until my vision cleared.

"Don't cry, please. I don't blame you for this. I'd rather you held my reins than anyone, but—"

"A slave is still a slave."

We'd discussed this moment since we were old enough to understand the circumstances of our births. The complex tangle of lies and blood made Emma a slave while our elder half-sister, Nesvia, was first in line for the throne. She was the only child born to my mother and Emma's father, and virtually a stranger to us both.

Since our monarchy was matriarchal, my birth had been acknowledged and my title secured.

Emma's mother had been a young serving girl turned courtesan around the time of Nesvia's birth, when Archer's choice of marital activities was severely limited. Though Emma shared half Nesvia's blood, she would forever be in service to the royal house, and because of that, to me.

"Yes," she agreed. "A slave is still a slave."

A new voice entered our conversation. "And a slave should always know her place, which is not bemoaning her station to her mistress. No matter how indulgent she may be."

The rustle of heavy fabric sliding over stones announced my mother's arrival. She wore turquoise gauze gathered at her shoulder with a silver broach to make a gown. Intricate tattoos covered her exposed skin, wrapping down and around the slender curve of her hip. Her shimmering skin looked dusted by fine diamond glitter. In all likelihood, it was.

"Madelyn, my dear, you look lovely," she cooed, stepping around my nude body in a slow half circle.

Until my skin dried, there was little point in wearing clothing. The gel would only ruin the lavender silk robe draped across the foot of my bed. Mother had also sent the matching pair of slippers with ribbons for my hair as a gift. In return, she expected perfection. And I had to deliver.

"Thank you, Mother." My swimming eyes fought to keep track of her languid perusal.

She clasped her hands eagerly. "Have you accepted any suitors?" She smiled coyly. "I know you haven't lacked for attention. The males of First Court have had their eyes on you for quite some time. Did their solicitations arrive promptly?"

"Yes, I have received their mailings." Bags of queries filled with tokens of esteem and empty promises for pleasure I had no interest in tasting had been arriving steadily for weeks. "But I have decided against accepting their very generous offers."

I had, however, accepted another offer. Or I would when next I saw Archer. As much as I abhorred the idea of taking anything from him, agreeing to his demands would yield the greatest return. If I had to sell myself, I would take everything I could get to secure Emma's and Harper's futures.

Her mercurial temper flared in an instant. "Is this about that Evanti? Again?" Her eyes narrowed to thin slits. "You cannot lie with him. Not even tonight. Who knows what might happen?"

"Sex?" Emma supplied.

Mother stalked to Emma's side and leaned down to her ear. "Your virtue only matters until the ceremony's completion. Then your purity will no longer be an issue." Her fingernail trailed the curve of Emma's jaw, over the thick, pulsing artery in her neck. Blood beaded in the wake of her finger. "You would do well to remember that any males Madelyn turns away tonight will be looking to take their pleasure...elsewhere." Her promissory tone made Emma's fists ball at her sides.

She dismissed Emma and returned her attention to me. Her mood lightened just as quickly as it had soured. "No one thought conception between the two demon houses was possible." Her lips quirked upward in satisfaction I failed to understand. "Until you, it had never happened before. So, you will stay out of the beds of the Evanti until we decide how to make the best use of your unique...attributes."

The herbal concoction I'd downed earlier threatened to make an appearance. If Mother remained where she stood, it would likely splatter across her costly gown. Imagining the consequences, I swallowed convulsively. "I have no plans to take anyone to my bed tonight." The bitter lie coated my tongue. "I have rescinded those offers extended to me and wish to remain sequestered in my suite at the ceremony's end."

"You must make yourself available if you wish to secure a proper consort."

"Propriety doesn't matter to me." I was proving that tonight, wasn't I?

"It *is* that Evanti, isn't it?" she snarled, flashing from regal to rabid again in an instant. Spittle dotted her lush red lips. "You think to save yourself for him? A slave? Giving him to you as a guardian was second in stupidity only to allowing Archer's halfling bastard to remain in your service."

She paced without her characteristic grace, seeming to stomp her feet in tantrum with every step. "I have to wonder if my beloved Archer didn't make plans for this eventuality, although how it benefits him I can't imagine."

But I could. Giving Emma into my service lent him the illusion of propriety, whereas her absence would have made his frequent jaunts to the otherwise empty summer castle suspect.

Mother was a whirlwind of turquoise storming across my

room. I had never seen her so riled. Her normally blunt nails lengthened as a spark verging on insanity brightened her eyes. She was out for blood and I feared whom she had chosen to sacrifice.

I made my choice in an instant. "I'm sorry to have distressed you." I swallowed the bile rising in my throat and shoved down a sob threatening to break the straight lines of my posture. "If it pleases you, you may pick a male to enter my rooms tonight."

This lie came much more readily to my lips. I knew it would be her consort attending me instead. Archer had plotted too carefully not to have anticipated a similar contingency. He would have ways of dealing with errant suitors seeking the bed he planned to occupy for the night.

Mother preened, placated at once by my show of deference. I shivered as disgust slithered over my skin at the thought of allowing her horrid life partner the use of my body. The reality of Archer made the offer of an anonymous male seem almost appealing.

"Dear," she crooned, brushing her mouth with the tips of her fingers. "Being second born doesn't mean you have to lower your standards." She smiled grimly. "If something were to happen to your sister before her prime, then you would rule in her stead."

"Rideal will never allow a hair on his wife's head to be harmed. Nesvia will wear the crown as is her birthright."

My brother by marriage, Rideal, was broad of shoulder and dull of wit, but he loved his wife with single-minded determination. No one would reach her through him. Of that I was certain.

Another sigh of disappointment from Mother had Emma rolling her eyes behind the queen's back.

"You never were very ambitious."

I painted on a false smile. "I'm sorry my disinterest in court politics offends you. I regret that my unwillingness to help you prolong your own reign embitters you towards me."

Mother chuckled. "Little one, if I decide I'm unwilling to relinquish my throne, I'll snap Nesvia's neck with my own two hands." She turned serious. "That kind of coup must be witnessed, you know. Otherwise there would be gossip as to whether I still had the stomach for such things after my centennial." Her eyes cut to me. "Especially after your birth. I've endured much controversy over my decision to allow you to live, even secluded as you have been in Rihos." A secret smile played around her lips before she sobered. "Spin around, let me see your back."

I turned gingerly, trying to keep my balance as the room listed around me.

"Your hair," she ordered. "Lift it."

I gathered the strands in my sticky fingers as best I could. My hands were numb, useless appendages requiring visual aid to function. I relied on the mirror to show me what I couldn't feel.

Mother swallowed audibly. "Oh, Zaniah preserves us. I'd forgotten how horrible they look." In the mirror's reflection, I saw the color draining from her cheeks. Hands fluttering, she caught Emma's attention. "See to it that those...things are covered before her presentation."

Under Mother's disgusted glare, the nubs seemed to move of their own accord, as if flexing the wings she'd had amputated and proving they were a valid, integral part of me. She gagged and staggered back, shielding her eyes with a hand. "Drop your hair. Drop it!"

The length of my hair fell down to the high curve of my

bottom, completely concealing my back. As I turned to face her, she muttered, "Hideous things."

I couldn't argue when I felt the same exact way.

The harsh click of boot on stone announced Archer's arrival. His smug expression spoke volumes about his confidence in my acceptance of his offer.

"The court is alive with anticipation, my dears." Archer barged into the room and pushed past Emma like the king he pretended his marriage made him. "Never has an ascendant drawn such a gathering. Appropriate fanfare for our beautiful Madelyn, I must say."

His expression softened, taking in my appearance with glittering eyes and a quick lick of his bottom lip. Chill bumps dotted my skin as his gaze swung towards Mother, who watched his antics with a slight curl of her lip.

"Now, Eliya," he said when he noticed her expression. "You mustn't blame Madelyn for the sins of her mother. You should have considered the repercussions of bedding an Evanti if you didn't want a child born with their defects."

"Madelyn is not defective." Emma's chilled voice swept through the room. "Why must you revel in making her believe there's something wrong with her?"

"Have you never seen her back?" Archer spun towards his daughter while his laughter boomed in my ears. "She is a beautiful placeholder for the crown and that is all she'll ever be. A court intrigue with a disgusting abnormality that will attract the eager and curious."

Emma took a step closer. "How can you speak to her that way? She is your daughter, in name if not by blood."

Archer clearly didn't relish the reminder. He took a step towards Emma to match the one she'd taken towards him.

"I am not her father." He looked to me, seeking assurance he held my attention. "Would you like me to tell you about her sire?"

I braced myself against the story he was so eager to retell. Flashes of my nighttime terrors filled my mind. Perhaps I knew their source after all. His story, retold in clarion detail, haunted me.

"Eliya wished to punish me for your birth. I'd bedded a courtesan, so she took the next step down—her Evanti guardian." His grin bared wicked teeth. "You can imagine her surprise to learn she'd been seeded, something always thought to be impossible. In her rage, she ordered me to sever her guardian's wings on the day Madelyn's conception was confirmed. I told Eliya to rid herself of the abomination, but after careful consideration, she thought it a novelty and wanted to do something that had never been done." He laughed indulgently. "I left her lover bound in the courtyard and forced him to watch my wife swell with his child." His tone turned reflective. "When Madelyn was born, and I plucked the satin wings from her back, he fell to his knees and begged me to cut out his heart. As I did, he thanked me for it."

"Zehiel," I said softly. "My father's name was Zehiel." As a child, I had longed for some connection to my real father, and Harper had given it to me in the form of that single word. My breath hitched and a film covered my eyes, blurring everyone and everything into watery outlines.

Mother slapped Archer hard across the face. I think all three of us jerked in surprise at her sudden outburst. He lifted a hand to his cheek reverently, as if she'd given him a gift instead of calling him to heel.

"You fool." She glowered, stabbing the air in my direction. "Look at her. You've made her cry. She can't be splotchy during her presentation, I won't have it."

Emma stepped to my side. Her nearness soothed me.

"My lady, I will see to Madelyn's final preparations."

"Final preparations" sounded appropriate since a part of me would never return to these familiar suites. What little innocence I had left wouldn't linger far beyond the return to my bedroom door.

Archer went to Mother's side and wrapped a hand around the base of her skull, crushing his lips to hers in a brutal kiss. "See, my love? All is well." He pulled away, grinning with the sheen of blood smeared across his bottom lip. Whether his or hers, I didn't know. The rouge of her lips concealed any wound she might have gotten, and I felt it far more likely she'd given instead.

"My Queen." He bowed low in a courtly gesture. "It's time for us to enter the hall. Your court anxiously awaits you."

Mother allowed him to take her arm, casting one last glance at me as she neared the threshold. "Today is the first day of the life you were born to lead. Embrace it, and all will be well."

I watched her go and wished that I could believe her.

Chapter Three

Emma had left me moments earlier holding a cold compress to my eyes, hoping to draw out the redness left from my crying jag. Behind the soft cloth my world was a dark and empty place, peaceful. How I wished I could remain there.

A few dull thumps fell in the distance. Almost like the sound of bare footsteps on stone.

"Hello?"

No one answered. I waited and heard the noise again, louder and growing closer.

I lowered the rag in time to see a blond male jog up the last two stairs in the hall and sweep into my room with casual familiarity.

A flush crept up my neck, tingling at the base of my skull. I wore only a pair of lavender slippers with matching ribbons braided through my hair. Not that he'd noticed. He didn't even glance my way.

Maybe he'd been warned not to upset me in light of Archer's mishap. Or maybe his aversion was for more aesthetic reasons.

I almost told him my back was covered and he need not fear what he would see, but I didn't really want to invite his attention, did I?

As I admired the straight line of his back and purposeful stride, I thought maybe I did want validation from this male. He seemed so self-assured when I wasn't sure of anything. Both the choices I'd made and the life I lived were things I found myself able to forget as I watched his slow circuit of my room.

I appraised him while his attention was otherwise engaged. The way his bloused ivory shirt and matching vest were unadorned but seemed to hug his body as if tailored for him. His white breeches had minimal gold trim with the cuff banded just above his muscular calves.

I couldn't seem to look away from him.

He lifted my robe and held it out at arm's length. I couldn't see his face from this angle, but his chuckle sounded less than reassuring.

Then fear set in, racing up my spine and freezing me in place. What if this was the male Mother had chosen? Could he even now be surveying my rooms while he planned his conquest?

"You shouldn't be up here."

He didn't answer, but he did stand still.

"I must insist that you leave," I said crisply. "You will be punished if you're found in my rooms."

He glanced up then, and his full black eyes peered out at me from a somewhat familiar face.

"Harper?" I gasped. "Is that really you?" I couldn't stop the sudden, unexpected laughter from bubbling out of me. "You haven't used glamour in ages."

Not since we'd been children and he'd wanted to look as I did. He'd said if I couldn't have my wings, then he hadn't wanted his either, but that had been before he learned to fly.

The bittersweet memory curved my lips.

I couldn't stop from going to him and running my fingers through his shaggy hair or resting my hand against his olive-toned skin. "It's a nice look for you." I giggled again.

He held the robe out to me, helping me slip my arms through the sleeves. I still shook with silent laughter as he tied the belt around my waist. When he pulled away, his lips were thin and disapproving. "Could you please stop laughing at me?"

I pinched my lips together tightly.

"Very good." He winked at me through thick black lashes as he dropped into a formal bow.

Stopping with one leg outstretched, he made a show of picking invisible lint from his hosiery before looking back up to me. "My lady, would you allow me the honor of acting as your escort this evening?"

I dropped into a curtsey opposite him, lifting imaginary skirts while fluttering my eyelashes in what I hoped was a provocative manner.

"I would be honored to arrive on your arm, my lord." I offered my hand to him.

He took it and reeled me against him too hard so that our chests bumped together.

Then our eyes met and his gaze lowered to my mouth. But just when our lips would have touched, he shifted his angle and kissed my cheek instead, like always.

I'd spent ample time wondering how it would feel to have his lips pressed to mine in a real kiss. Soft and warm, I imagined. Possibly tasting sweetly of the dates he liked to eat. While I was eager to learn, he seemed unwilling to educate me in such matters.

I blamed his reluctance on concerns about propriety.

The moment's levity passed as reality set in. This was going to happen. It had to happen, but acknowledging the fact made little difference while standing on the precipice of change.

"Ask me to take you away from all of this." His mouth found my ear. "Please."

This proud male who never asked for anything was asking me to save myself, but I couldn't. Not unless I was willing to bargain my life for his, and I wasn't.

"Shh." I tucked my face in the bend of his neck and ran my hands over the taut muscles in his back. "The ceremony will only last for a few hours and then we can all put this behind us."

His thick and lovely fingers burrowed beneath my hair. "I don't know if I'm strong enough to know this is happening and not try to stop it."

For a second, I thought he meant the deal I planned to make with Archer, but his tone held only quiet sadness instead of the banked rage it would have had he known. I pressed a kiss to his jaw. "Emma and I..."

His gaze broke from mine to scan the bedroom. "Where is she?"

"They've already taken her down to the great hall."

His arms slipped from around my shoulders as he backed away, eyes wild and flashing from ebony to silver.

I captured his face between my hands. "It's all right. We all knew this day would come."

He gripped my shoulders, and his nails dug into my skin. "I can't do this. I can't let this happen and pretend it's okay because it isn't." His voice rose steadily until my ears hurt from the pitch. "This is torture cloaked under the guise of some archaic rite of passage."

"We'll all come out of this on the other side. I promise." I hoped I offered him the truth. "In a few hours all of this will be over. Mother and her court will leave. Archer will too, at least for a while. Then things will be as they always have been."

I failed to mention my eventual consort, assuming Archer ever freed me to find one. I didn't want to think about it, and Harper's evident misery proved neither did he.

His head jerked in unsteady nods. "Of course." His voice broke. "You're right. Forgive me."

I looped my arm through his. "It's hard to see those you love hurt when there's nothing you can do to ease their pain."

His eyes became distant before pulling in to focus on me. "I would do anything, give anything, to save you both from this. But you won't let me, will you?"

"No." I straightened his shirt collar one-handed. "Nothing can save us from fate."

I took the first, unwilling step towards the door. Harper didn't follow until the final second when my arm would have pulled free of his.

I flashed him a nervous smile. "Ready?"

His crooked grin made a brief appearance. "I should be asking you that."

"Well, I am. Let's get this over with, shall we?"

We walked arm in arm through the hallways joining my suite to the rest of the castle, down the long and murky tunnel leading into the public spaces, then finally to the arched entrance of the great hall.

It seemed Archer hadn't exaggerated. I'd never seen so many nobles gathered in one place. Granted, summer court was the only gathering I ever witnessed. And it occurred at the low point of the social calendar, at a time when most nobles doffed their transient ways and went home to their own estates. Only then did Mother come here.

The hall held standing-room-only spectators, all dressed in richly colored velvets and other court finery. All tried to outdo their neighbor in the silent contest to see whose portrayal of boredom rang with the most authenticity.

They must have closed ranks against any commoners seeking to join in the festivities. If I'd pricked the finger of each demon present, the welling drop would have been a vibrant blue.

The chattering of the crowd ceased all at once. Their dull expressions lit with interest as they saw me poised to enter on Harper's arm. A woman on the outmost fringes pointed in our direction, but I had the strangest feeling her finger was aimed at him rather than me.

He stopped me from taking the first step. "Say the word, and I will take you away from this place."

I squeezed his arm lightly. "There's nowhere for us to go, nowhere safe. And I could never leave Emma behind."

"Neither could I. The three of us, we could leave. You don't have to do this."

"There is no other choice." I prayed he didn't learn of the deal I would make until I held his papers in my hand.

I took the first step and entered the hall to a sickening wave of applause that rumbled through the stones beneath my feet.

Harper came to my side reluctantly and guided me towards the elevated dais centered against the far wall. Mother sat highest, with Archer seated to her left and Nesvia to her right.

Rideal stood, a silent sentry, just behind his wife's chair, scanning the crowd without settling on any one face for too long. Nesvia stroked the hand resting on her shoulder fondly.

I pulled my arm from Harper's hold and took the short stairs to my place beside Nesvia. He waited until I had completed my climb before turning to leave.

Before he took a single step, two guards appeared, wearing identical, full-court glamour. They caught him, one each around his biceps, but instead of leading him outside, they dragged him front and center into the crowd.

My gaze snapped to Mother. "Slaves are never allowed to witness the ceremony. What is the meaning of this?"

"Entertainment," Archer replied for her, pointing. "And assurance that any of your later plans will go uninterrupted."

I followed his finger and saw what he'd meant. The guards half dragged Harper towards one of the stone support pillars. The assembly cleared, revealing chains coiled and gleaming around the base of the marble column.

"What will you do to him?" I asked, striving to project cool indifference while my heart burned.

"Make sure he realizes you belong to Askara, to the crown, and not with the likes of him," Archer said. "He should feel honored. Few Evanti ever witness such a momentous occasion."

The center of my chest cooled. This had been his plan all along. I could see that now. None of us had escaped unscathed yesterday. Archer had indulged his own anticipation, choosing to savor his victory today.

The pair of guards struggled to keep their hold on Harper as they wound the thick chains around his chest and secured his hands behind him. When his head snapped up, his eyes shone silver and feral, passing over me to stare into the hallway opposite the one where we'd entered.

I followed his line of sight to where Emma stood, waiting for her cue. From the corner of my eye, I saw Mother motion her forward with a quick flick of her thin wrist.

My fingers dug into the armrest of my chair with palms so sweaty they almost slipped off the rounded edges. Emma winked at me before padding quietly forward. She stopped just before the dais and dropped her robe from her shoulders. Her fair skin grew flush from the heat of the room. With her shoulders back and spine straight, she faced us.

I had never wanted anything as badly as I wanted to be by her side, able to face this spectacle together instead of treading the line of propriety that ultimately would fail us both. Servant and mistress, we both would bleed the same.

Shifting my focus from Emma, I noted the stooped shadow lurking just outside the hall.

"Ah, good priest, you've kept us waiting." Mother smiled, waving the hunchback male forward.

My stomach roiled as the priest entered the hall with shuffling steps, dragging a creaking cart full of supplies in his wake. He stopped just behind Emma and rolled out a thin black drop cloth, instructing her to lie down upon it.

A low growl filled my ears, drawing my attention back to Harper. His face clouded with some foreign emotion as his gaze settled on Emma. When he looked up, I gasped at the depth of despair reflected at me.

I wanted to go to him, assure him everything would be all right. That this would soon be over and none of us ever had to remember again.

I should have taken his offer to escape and found those responsible for the missing Evanti. I could have begged or bartered our passage to wherever they had gone. Even with nowhere to run and the uncertainty that anyone would hide us, I should have fought back, should have done something besides folding under Archer's demands.

Emma's screech of pain startled me back to attention. She

writhed on the floor, held down by a guard pinning each limb while forcing her submission. An instrument similar to a quill pen was poised in the gnarled hand of the priest. The metallic sheen of gold flashed as he looked to Mother for permission, which she granted with a singular nod.

The priest stabbed the sharpened quill into Emma's cheek and began to inscribe proof of ownership onto her body.

When it was over, lavender runes covered her lovely face in a labyrinth of agonizingly beautiful patterns. I couldn't speak or move. Emma's body shook with sobs as her face swelled and bled onto the black mat beneath her.

The priest packed away his pen and exposed wizened flesh as he shoved his robe's sleeves up his arms to free his hands. A grim smile of expectation hovered around his twisted lips.

"My Queen, I would examine the handmaiden, Emmaline Gray, to ensure her virtue is intact and that she is fit to serve her mistress."

"No." I gained my feet. Things had gone too far. Tradition and Archer be damned, I couldn't sacrifice my sister to secure an uncertain future. I had thought I could bear this, but I was wrong. I couldn't stand by, placid and proper, while watching her suffer.

"You have to stop this, Mother, *now*."

Disappointment marred her perfect features before the tiny show of emotion slipped beneath her usual mask of impassivity. She gestured to the priest below. "Proceed," she said flatly.

He didn't have the chance to touch Emma again.

The walls of the great hall shook, calling everyone's attention to where a third of the evening's entertainment wrestled within the confines of his chains. The pillar strapped to Harper's back lurched from its base, sending bits of stone falling from the ceiling into the crowd below.

The court erupted into chaos.

The nobility's cries echoed around the hall as the links holding Harper stretched and distorted, falling into a misshaped pile at his feet. His glamour faded and his wings thrust outward, brightening with his fury until they shone vibrant red. His silvery eyes reflected the flurry of panicked guests trying to escape.

Mother's private guards surrounded her, ushering her through a passage hidden just behind her throne. She fled behind Nesvia, who stumbled along as Rideal dragged her to safety.

Only Archer stayed behind.

"I won't let him have you." Archer shoved me down, pinning me to the floor beneath him. "You were willing to make the deal." He tore aside my robe. "I saw acceptance in your face, and you will satisfy our bargain."

If death had a sound, I heard it then, passing through the open lips of the Evanti charging towards us. His guttural promise, a roar that splintered my soul and his, that everyone present would pay.

Harper cleared the dais in a single leap and slammed his shoulder into Archer's side, rolling them both off the carpeted edge to the stone floor below.

The grunts and growls of male combat filled my ears as I crawled away from the fray and found my way to Emma's side. She had sat upright after the priest scurried into an alcove, tugging her robe back into place, but hadn't moved otherwise. Her face was down-turned with her focus centered on the floor between her feet.

"Emma?"

When her head tilted up, searching for the sound of my voice, I saw why she hadn't moved. Her face was swollen and bruised; the fine web of tattoos crept across her skin. Her eyelids were puffy and closed. I doubted she could see anything. Even her lips were edged in pale purple and useless.

She tried to answer me, but couldn't.

"It's all right. You don't have to say anything." I took her hand in mine. "I'm here now and we're going to take you someplace safe."

Her fervent mumblings had my mind searching for her meaning.

"Harper?" I asked.

She squeezed my fingers in acknowledgment.

"He's fine." I twisted around to find him. "He's right over...there." When I located him, I almost wished I hadn't. "Oh, Zaniah, no," I whispered.

Harper and Archer's battle had progressed. Their chests heaved for air, each struggling to maintain the upper hand. Harper bared his teeth in a frenzied snarl, too wide and sharp to be the smile he projected.

I realized then that he enjoyed the way his fists met with failing resistance. Even his eyes glowed as he pummeled Archer almost unconscious. His expression shifted again, his lips curving back, brows drawing down. As if he'd come to some decision Archer hadn't yet reached.

I watched it all in slow motion. Sound became distant and fuzzy. Everything ceased to be except for the large palm Harper wrapped around Archer's face. The point of no return came and went as Harper slammed Archer's head against the unforgiving stone floor in a single, downward thrust.

My eyes closed but couldn't block out the sound, dense and succulent, like the death of a ripe melon.

Harper stood and turned from the corpse. His long strides

consumed the ground between us.

When he saw Emma's face, he dropped to his knees beside her and encircled her with his arms and wings. I saw him whispering to her but couldn't hear the words and wasn't meant to. They were an assurance just for her.

Fierce determination burned in his eyes as he gathered Emma and stood. "We have to leave this place. Please, if you care for your sister or me at all, you'll come with us."

My thoughts jumbled, grasping on one certainty. If we stayed, Harper would be hanged. Emma...I couldn't think about what would be done to her just yet. I couldn't let this all be for nothing. If we stopped now, it would all begin again. I couldn't let that happen.

I gave the only answer. "Lead the way."

He almost smiled. "If we can get to the courtyard, I think I can fly us out of here."

I didn't want to do the math of one set of wings times the weight of three bodies. I wanted to know where we would go, but I had to run flat out to keep up with him and had no breath for questions.

We took a winding path from the great hall that led out into the open air. I could hear the low hum of voices approaching. The driving beat of feet falling in urgent pursuit.

"We have to leave *now*. The guards are coming." I didn't have to remind him of how accurate the archers were, or that one errant arrow could slice his wings and end our escape before it began.

I didn't have to, but if he didn't move soon, I would.

"Give me a second to shift, Emma." I heard her soft whimper just before his arms wound around me, lifting me up almost onto his hip. "You'll have to hold on tight, and still this might not work. I've never flown two before."

I held tight and prayed as his wings unfurled and labored to get us airborne.

After a time, his downward strokes became less strained. His arms quivered around me, but his grip never loosened and our course never veered. My chin kept dropping to his shoulder, though I tried to keep watch in case we were followed.

"You can close your eyes. I know my way."

I wanted to ask how, but given his permission, my mind drifted. The last thing I heard was the soft chuckle of his exhausted laughter beneath my ear.

Chapter Four

Harper's wide shoulder rolled beneath my cheek. "We're here." His gruff voice finished the job of rousing me from a sound sleep.

My eyes opened to darkness. "Where is *here*?"

I blinked several times, but my vision didn't improve. I held Harper closer as my chest tightened and pulse quickened. Only his warmth beneath my fingers anchored me in the vast and blinding night. I realized then our journey had lasted long enough for the affects of the anesthetic to dissipate. Several hours of travel at least.

"You don't have to be afraid." His thumb stroked my back. "Everything is all right. We're back on solid ground. Everyone is asleep. That's why there's no light."

"I'm not afraid." I released him from my death grip.

He laughed. "I never said you were."

"You never said where we were, either."

"You'll see," he said with a smile in his voice. I felt his lungs expand before he called into the empty night, "*Tergath nor. I seek safe haven.*"

I was surprised when a child's voice answered back.

"*Tergath norta,*" the timid voice replied. "There is no safe haven."

The exchange seemed to be a code of some kind. But that made no sense because he knew what to say. Which meant he must have been here before, but why? How?

The sound of his outright laughter jarred me. "Marisol, leave the watch to your elders and fetch Dana."

"Yes, sir." A soft sigh, already fading away, punctuated her petulant response.

"Put me down." I struggled in Harper's hold, but he only tightened his grip on me. I wanted distance he refused to allow. Questions poured out of me. "How do you know her name? What is this place? Where have you taken us?"

"Stop fighting me before you hit Emma. You'll only hurt yourself if I put you down now," he said. I stilled, reluctant to admit he had a point. "Give it just a moment longer."

Bright lights flooded the area where we stood and allowed my greedy gaze to drink in our surroundings. I raised a hand to shelter my eyes from the glare as Harper slid me down his side.

"What is this place?"

My slippers had fallen off at some point during the flight. When my feet touched the ground, they met blades of cool, soft grass. Trees with lengthy green needles spiking from their branches encircled us. Everything looked so lush and alive when compared to the harsh desert clime of Rihos.

"This is an Evanti colony," he answered. "The only one of its kind."

I faced him, startled by the wealth of knowledge in his voice. "You knew about this place?"

His heavy sigh concerned me.

"I have a lot of explaining to do." His fingertips trailed my arm. "I never imagined I would have the chance to show you the colony. It's so full of possibilities. We can all build better lives here, together."

I latched onto the most critical point—he meant to stay with us. The rest could be pulled into perspective once this new world stopped spinning around me.

Behind us, a door opened and closed with a sharp click, drawing our attention.

"Is that you, Harper? I didn't expect to see you back so soon." A feminine shape broke through the outer fringes of the pooling light. "Marisol said you brought guests?"

Squinting against the glare, I saw she stood on a wooden platform attached to a small house a few yards away. She came forward, cradling her distended stomach with one hand.

The woman stopped a few steps away as her pale blue gaze washed over Emma and me. What might have started as a smile faded as she glanced quickly back to Harper. "What have you done?"

"I've killed the Askaran Queen's consort and kidnapped a princess," he said, then gestured to each of us in turn. "Dana Evans, this is Princess Madelyn DeGray and her sister, Emmaline Gray."

Dana massaged her temples. "You never do things by half, do you?"

He grimaced in response. "Where are Marcus and Clayton?"

"They've gone on a recovery mission." Her hand smoothed across her rounded belly. "I don't expect them back for at least another week."

"Their timing is flawless, as usual." Buried in the sharp words I heard respect, maybe affection.

My head ached from the questions lobbying around my brain. Was no one else lost? Confused? Did no one else wonder how Harper had known to come here?

I interrupted their casual banter. "I don't understand. How do you know these people? Where is this colony?"

Harper took a shaky step forward, trembling from exhaustion and still laboring under Emma's unconscious weight.

"I've brought you to the earthen realm." He reached for me, but I stepped back a second time. "This colony is where our children are raised and our women are kept safe. It had to remain a secret."

The words burst from my lips. "Even from me?" Immediately, I wished they hadn't.

"Especially from you."

"Oh." It was the best reply I could manufacture in response to the line he'd drawn between us. I cleared my throat and pretended interest in Dana.

"So this is the earthen realm?" I took in her sleep-tousled appearance and the soft pink gown that fell just below her knees. "I've never seen a human outside of Rihos." Dana shielded her stomach when she noticed it held my attention. "Are you breeders?"

She chuckled and wiggled a finger in the air. The bright lights glinted from a small stone set in a band around her finger. "We marry here, hon. Nothing happens without full consent of both partners. We're making families, trying to give our males the lives and peace they deserve."

Harper braced a hand on my shoulder as he spoke. "Forgive her. Maddie's only left the summer castle a half dozen times in her life. She doesn't know any better."

Heat rushed through my cheeks. I knew I was naïve, but to hear him say it...as if he were making excuses for a small child. I took a step back and wished the shadows could conceal me.

"I had no idea." Dana laid a hand over her heart. "I've never met an Askaran before. We've only heard stories from the men...and they aren't pretty."

"No," I agreed. "I don't suppose they would be."

"Dana." Harper shifted Emma from his shoulder and into his arms. "Do you have a room we can use?"

"Oh, I don't know where my mind has gone. Hormones I guess." She waved us on, stepping into the shadows of a doorway. "Come on, I always keep the spare ready just in case."

He followed as far as the door before turning to locate me. "Are you coming?" He tucked Emma closer to squeeze through the narrow entrance.

Standing in the grass, I was surrounded by an alien world in the center of a colony I'd never dreamed existed. Harper was my lifeline, the one thing left to me that still made sense.

I nodded and tightened my robe to ward off the slight chill I hadn't noticed in my confusion.

Indoors, an overwhelming floral scent tickled my nose and made me sneeze. We walked through a gloomy hallway, and I ran my hands down either side of the textured walls to keep my balance. Our hostess led us into a small room occupied by a large canopied bed and filled with an assortment of simple but matching furniture.

Patterned quilts lay folded in perfect stacks at the foot of the bed. Harper knocked them aside as he lowered Emma. She jerked awake when her back contacted the mattress, her unfocused eyes searching the room until they lit on me. Then her shoulders slumped and she sank into her pillow.

Waving a hand, Emma called me over to her. I crawled onto the soft bed and straightened her robe to cover her better.

"How do you feel?" I asked, relieved the swelling had gone

down enough for her eyes to open and her lips to part on a pained exhale.

"Like my face was trampled by horses...with razor blades embedded in their hooves."

Her admission ripped through me like a punch to my gut.

"I should have done something, said something. I could have tried harder to stop them. I could have refused Archer's offer outright."

Her arm wound around my hip. "If I hadn't been so determined to prove I could take whatever Father threw at me, I would have saved myself." She gave me a squeeze. "We escaped. Nothing else matters." She looked up to Harper. "Are we safe here?"

He nodded. "I'll need to speak with Marcus. He's the male in charge. Adjustments will have to be made, permissions granted, but the colony is well protected. If he chooses to offer you asylum, the queen won't find you here."

"But she will try," I said, certain of that at least.

He tousled his hair with a careless hand, aiming a question at Dana. "How long did you say they would be gone?"

"Another week at least."

That same hand smoothed down his face, which was creased by deep worry lines.

"Perfect timing," he muttered again. "We can't risk Marcus or Clayton, or the others, and they'll have no way of knowing what I've done until it's too late." His arms crossed over his chest. "I have to get word to them. They have to know what's happened and that the stakes have been raised."

Dana turned to leave. "I'll call Demetrius. He's out of rotation this month, but he won't mind making the trip to carry your message." Her teeth worried her bottom lip. "I think we'd all sleep better knowing the others had been warned."

He caught her lightly by the elbow. "No, it's my mess, and I'll clean it up." His troubled eyes sought mine. "I have to ask you to trust me. Can you do that?"

I felt my eyes widen with the onset of dread. His voice had turned pleading, and it frightened me. "You know I trust you."

Already he looked relieved. "I know it's a lot to ask, but I need to do this. Marcus and Clayton are...very important to me. I'd never forgive myself if they came to harm because of my impulsiveness." He paused. "I'm asking you both to stay here for a few days. Just long enough for me to relay a message and come home."

Home, he said. As if it was the most natural thing in the world. Perhaps to him it was.

"You're leaving us." I tried to keep level and calm instead of giving in to the churning fear consuming me at the thought of being left here alone without him. He might know and trust these strangers, but they were no one and nothing to me.

"I'll only be gone for a few days. When I come home, we'll talk. I'll answer any questions you have for me."

Emma's fingers tightened on the limp fabric of my robe. I didn't want to be left behind either, but what choice did we have?

"You should go," she said. "If our escape endangered the lives of others, then we're not so selfish that we would keep you here to play nursemaid."

"She's right," I agreed. "You have to go. We'll be fine until you get back."

He flashed us a grateful smile and rested his hand on Dana's shoulder, turning serious as he spoke to us. "You are currently guests of the Evans Inn, which is Dana's contribution to the colony. She also handles registration for all new colonists." He turned to her. "Pull out the holdings' log and let's get them set up."

She held up her pointer to signal she needed a moment then stepped out into the hall. "Let me run over to the office. I'll be right back."

Furniture scraped in the room next door as a chair slid over uncovered flooring.

We were left alone with Harper, whose attention already seemed focused elsewhere. He pulled a scrap of leather from his pocket and wrapped it around his wrist. I recognized the bracelet I'd made him years earlier with each of our names worked into the beading. He often wore it for luck.

He fumbled the hooked closure and, glancing up, his eyes met mine. His gaze softened. My lips compressed until they throbbed. It wasn't pleasant, but neither were any of the words waiting to escape if my mouth were to open.

"Don't look at me that way. You don't understand. There are so many more lives at stake besides our own. It wasn't my place to make this decision. I would have—"

"Found them." Dana pushed back into the room, waving two thick stacks of paper housed between a pair of multicolored folders. She glanced between the three of us. "Should I wait outside?"

He answered her before I could. "No, please. I want to know Maddie and Emma are settled in before I leave. We'll have plenty of time for answers later." He shot me a pointed look. "And don't think I didn't hear what you said to Emma. Though it hardly matters now, I think we both have confessions to make."

I nodded, wanting more than anything to find some distraction outside of the hurt making each breath harder for me to take than the last.

Luckily, Dana had a whole speech memorized and well rehearsed. She slipped something onto her face, a frame that hooked just behind her ears and enlarged her eyes behind twin circles of transparency. They looked to be a reading aid, though I doubted any detail, no matter the size, escaped her eager eyes.

"Each colony member is given lodging, a modest sum of cash and employment. The town here is pretty small, so choices are limited. Everything is on a first-come, first-served basis." She flipped open a vibrant blue folder, licked her thumb and shuffled through the pages. "Let's see what we have. The grocery store, salon and diner are all vacant." She looked over her rims at us. "If you don't mind working under someone, there are other options, but I thought you might enjoy establishing your own place here, given your...um...unique situation." She took the frames off and leaned closer, as if confiding. "I'm not saying you'd have any trouble, mind you. This is a very close community and we all want to help one another out, but we've never had Askarans seek shelter here. I just don't want to see anyone's feelings get hurt. That's all."

Beside me, Emma spoke through gritted teeth as she worked to sit upright. "How will we live if no one is willing to pay for our services?" Her earlier fog cleared as she shifted into survival mode. We sat shoulder to shoulder.

The simple contact with her reassured me. It helped me to remember even with Harper gone I wouldn't be alone. I would have Emma, and it would be enough.

"Oh, we have a decent amount of through traffic. We're sort of a truck-stop town. People come and go. We just do our best not to encourage them to stay." She smiled. "So you should be just fine."

Emma hummed low in her throat, considering. "We'll take

the diner. No matter their feelings for us, everyone has to eat. If you have an abundance of travelers, then our history will be a moot point." She bumped against me. "Does that sound all right with you?"

"Yes. Until we see what type of reception we receive, we need to focus on the necessities."

Emma tapped a finger stained with blood against the crisp, white paper held in Dana's hands. "The diner is what we'd like. How will this work?"

"Well, it's all fairly simple, really." Dana repeated the quick lick to her thumb and shuffled through a new stack of papers. "Clayton Delaney owns the property." She made a clucking sound with her tongue. "Since he's never here, I have power of attorney, so it won't be a big deal to make this all official in the morning."

"Will he mind you giving away his property?"

"Clayton?" She chuckled. "No, this is how it works for everyone. The town is our sanctuary. You'll only find Evanti, their wives and children here. We have the occasional human. Some even work in town, but they're mostly family members or are demon friendly." She glanced up. "Otherwise, like I said, we make sure passersby keep passing by, unless one of the males becomes interested." Her gaze shifted to Harper. "You know how they are when they set their mind to something. For such big and bad demons, they sure fall hard and fast."

She produced a marbled pen from her pocket and waved the uncapped end between me and Emma. "I assume you wish to live together?"

"Yes," we said in unison.

She flipped through another file and made notes. The fluorescent yellow folder made me squint and finally look away. I hoped obnoxious colors weren't the norm here.

Dana straightened. "We have temporary quarters you can use until a suitable home can be located." She rubbed slow circles in the small of her back. "As I said before, the town was quaint to begin with and our numbers keep growing. You might be cramped for a while, but we'll find somewhere you both like."

"Thank you for your kindness."

Emma repeated my sentiments.

"You're both very welcome." Dana went to stand by the door. "One more thing before I start processing your paperwork. Have you considered changing your last names?" She frowned. "It might help everyone forget faster if they aren't hearing the DeGray name or its derivatives thrown around."

I shrugged. "I'm not partial to my last name. It would be nice to share a common name with my sister."

Emma leaned back against her pillows and sighed tiredly. "I agree with any measures you think will keep Maddie safe."

Harper pushed from the wall. "Dana will see to it that neither of you are bothered." Walking over to the bed, he stooped down to press a kiss to my cheek, and then lifted Emma's hand to brush his lips across her knuckles. "I don't want to leave either of you this way, but every minute I'm here is time that good males are stumbling around blindly out there."

"We can entertain ourselves for a few days." I sighed, too exhausted to feel much of anything. "Don't worry about us."

He strode to the door and took the knob in his hand before looking back at us. "I love you, Maddie. No matter what else happens, know that."

Dana's jaw dropped open. She tucked the files as close to her chest as her stomach allowed. "I didn't realize...is she yours?"

Her curiosity fueled my own. My heart lodged in my throat as I waited to see if he would claim me as his.

His cocky grin made one final appearance. "She is my heart and always will be."

His sweet words soothed the worst of my anxieties. Whatever else he'd done or said, and wherever else he'd been, he had always come home to me.

I offered him a smile, and this time, I meant it. "Just be careful."

"As you wish, my lady," he teased.

Dana glowed. "Well, well. How the mighty have fallen." She followed him into the hall, pausing just outside the door. "Would you girls like me to leave the light on or off?" She glanced at a thin gold chain around her wrist. "It's around two a.m. here, so no one will be up for a few hours yet."

Emma's eyes had already closed. "Turn it off. Please."

I lay beside her, draping my arm over her waist and tucking it between her side and the mattress. Then the room went dark.

"Sweet dreams."

"Good night."

I snapped awake drenched in cold sweat. Throwing off the covers tangled around my waist, I had one foot on the hard floor before I realized where I was. Not home, but safe. The burst of anxious energy subsided until my ears filled with the wail of sirens piercing the night.

I jumped as an agonized scream rose from somewhere just beyond our room. Doors slammed open in the hall as the house awakened. Male voices called sharp orders and issued soothing words before leaving us in stilted silence.

The mattress shifted. Emma righted herself and closed her

strong fingers around my wrist, holding me in place.

"What do you think it means?"

Emma remained silent, but she almost vibrated with coiled anticipation. She swung her legs over the edge of the bed. "Stay here. I'll find Dana and ask what this is about." She paused. "And if we should be worried."

The door to our room swung open wide and filled with Dana's curvy silhouette. Her frantic hands pawed along the wall. A sharp click later and light bathed the room.

She panted deeply. "They're gone."

Pain contorted her features, washing the color from her face. She clutched her stomach with both hands and groaned hoarsely, leaning into the doorframe and sliding down to the carpeted floor. Her red nose sniffled and dark circles filled the hollows beneath both eyes.

"What do you mean, gone?" I asked. "Harper should have left hours ago."

A second woman arrived and bent down. Dana slapped away her hands. When a third woman came into view, they threaded their arms through Dana's and pulled her to her feet. When her breath caught on a sob, the room spun around me in dizzying circles. I broke Emma's hold as I went to my feet.

"What's happened?" I looked between the women. "What's wrong with Dana?"

"She's gone into shock," the woman on the left supplied.

To the right, the other woman added, "She's gone into labor. We have to get her to the hospital."

My skin prickled with awareness, and I turned to find Emma standing behind me. Her brow crinkled with thoughts and implications my fevered mind failed to grasp.

"What aren't you telling us?" Emma asked quietly.

Neither woman answered.

"The rescue party," Dana gasped. Her harsh breaths sawed in and out, shaking her petite frame with each unsteady gulp. "They heard about the ceremony... The guards were doubled... They were attacked on their way back to the colony."

Slipping boneless through the women's hands, she landed in a graceless sprawl across the floor with her body centered in a pool of pink fabric from her nightgown.

"They're dead." Her body quaked with her cries. Each sob caused violent spasms in her back. She bucked against the floor before curling into a ball on her side.

My feet guided me forward. "What about Harper?"

Dana didn't answer. I would have shaken the information from her if Emma hadn't stepped to my side and turned her attention from them to me.

"Where is Harper?" I shouted in order to be heard over her mewling. "*Where is he?*"

"He didn't come back," the woman on the right snapped. "We have three dead and two more males missing. Bodies they were unable to retrieve. Does that answer your question?"

I didn't realize I had charged them, only felt the weight of my sister anchoring me in place. My nails lengthened to black-tipped claws. I barely registered the sharp pressure of Emma locking my arms behind my back.

I charged again, fueled by my desperation to find Harper.

Emma anticipated me, forcing my elbow up until my wrist was level with my spine. Then she slammed me to the floor and pinned me beneath her.

"Stop it." Her knee dug into my lower back as her arms twined with mine in a hold I had no hope of breaking. Her hollow voice collapsed. "He's gone, *vinda koosh*. We've lost him."

"No! They're wrong!" I shrieked and thrashed beneath her. "I have to see him. I have to." I couldn't get enough air. I inhaled, felt my lungs expand against my ribs as if preparing to scream. Then I realized the sirens had stopped. The ear-piercing wails bouncing off the walls of the small room were mine.

"He can't be gone," I cried, lowering my head to the hardwood floor. "He can't be."

I think I stopped breathing.

Chapter Five

Earthen Realm, Five Years Later

Emma crossed our peeling front porch wearing fleece pajama bottoms tucked into heavy work boots. She huddled inside her quilted jacket, carrying a pair of mugs steaming a trail in her wake. "Madelyn Toliver, I want your butt back in the house this instant." Clouds of hot breath huffed out over her lips, suspending in the air between us.

"I'm almost ready to go inside." I dropped the book I'd been pretending to read for the last few hours on the wicker coffee table nudging my knees. The table and two chair set was courtesy of an end-of-season clearance sale at Home Depot the previous summer. Along with a few gallons of paint, the furniture represented our first purchases as homeowners.

She sank into the rocker beside me, and after a brief pause our chairs creaked in tandem. "Drink this." She pressed one of the mugs into my hands. "Extra marshmallows, just the way you like it."

The first sip of cocoa scalded the taste buds from my tongue. By the second gulp, I accepted the fact a week would pass before I would taste again.

"Do you see that white fluffy stuff?" Emma pointed towards an offending snowflake, tracking it with her finger until it drifted down to nestle among other equally offensive flakes littering our front steps.

"Yes." I took another drink, enjoying the way the hot chocolate twisted down to warm my insides. I snorted in the face of her sarcasm. "I think it's called snow."

Emma's eyes narrowed to thin slits. Glamour concealed her lavender scrollwork. She lifted her mug and blew across the steaming liquid, but lowered it without drinking. "It's freezing out here." Her gaze swept me from head to foot. "You do know that, right?"

I glanced down my body, checking to see if all my bases were covered. A petal-pink fleece jacket zipped just under my chin, covering a turtleneck sweater in the same shade. Starched denim encased my legs. I had even donned the pink crocheted cap Emma hung on a coat hook next to matching mittens dignity forbade me to wear even as far as my own porch.

I felt like one of those Barbie dolls the little girls from the colony favored—all pink and plastic.

Dressed by my sister's hands instead of an eight-year-old's, most days I could have doubled for the iconic figure since both of us relied on someone else's dreams to fulfill us, to make us real. I felt like my price tag was showing and the dollar amount found lacking. Her eyes were still on me. "What?"

"Your feet." Emma pointed. "I don't think I've ever seen them that lovely shade of blue before."

Numbness having nothing to do with the temperature had spread through my limbs hours earlier. I kicked out my foot, rotating my ankle back and forth as I admired the periwinkle hue. "Pretty."

She snatched my foot out of the air. "This is the kind of detail a human wouldn't overlook." She rubbed her hands, still warm from her cocoa, over my frozen skin. "A human would catch pneumonia or frostbite or something."

"I didn't notice it had gotten so cold."

Emma cocked one perfectly manicured brow. "You didn't notice your feet turning into blocks of ice?"

"No, I didn't." Pinpricks of discomfort spiked through my feet as blood began to sluggishly circulate. "Look, I'm sorry. I don't know what's wrong with me today."

Her sharp exhale ended on a sigh. "Yes, you do. We both do. Today makes five years since Harper...since he didn't come home. I know this day always knocks you for a loop, but there are things you need to—"

"Did you see that?" I leaned forward, staring down the road winding its way into town. Had I seen a flash of black against the whiteout? Flakes swirled by wings instead of wind?

Emma snapped her fingers an inch away from my nose. "Are you even listening to me?"

"I thought I saw something." A cyclone of snow twirled down the lane, forming a graceful, ghostly dancer. She stared at me, rather than the snow devil, which set my teeth on edge. "What?"

"Nothing." She smoothed her hands down her face as if I had made her tired instead of the late hour and long shift we'd both pulled today. "You can't keep going on like this; it's not good for you."

"I can take care of myself. I'm not the spoiled little princess from a faraway kingdom anymore."

"You never were." Her eyes mirrored my own ghosts. "You were the brave princess rescued from a nightmare by a handsome prince." She continued to rub my feet. "But it's been five years, and the other women are talking."

I picked at the crust of a dried marshmallow glued to the lip of my mug. "What are they saying?"

"They think you've been in mourning long enough." She ticked my offenses off with her fingers. "You only leave the house to work, you spend your days off hiking Emasen, you don't have any friends..." she saw my mouth open, "...and no, I'm your sister so I don't count. Everyone is worried about you."

"Why would they worry about me? I do my job and pay the tithes that support the colony. We're making progress in repaying the business loan from Mr. Delaney."

"See? That is my point exactly." Emma rested her hands across the flat tops of my feet. "It wasn't a loan we had to repay. The diner was a gift to help us begin our new lives with a purpose, a sense of ownership and belonging to this community. It's the reason we pay tithes in the first place."

"I don't want to owe anyone anything, certainly not some benevolent, faceless benefactor."

Emma snorted. "Clayton is hardly benevolent."

I shrugged. "I wouldn't know." Unless a person passed through the diner during my shift, they didn't rate a *ping* on my social radar. From everything I'd heard about Clayton Delaney, he made the kind of *ping* that turned heads, dropped jaws and required bibs to mop up drool having nothing to do with Emma's daily blackboard special.

During the five years I'd lived in the earthen realm, I had yet to cross paths with the illustrious Clayton, son of the deceased founder of the colony, Marcus Delaney. Since his father's death in the raid that cost me Harper, I had only interacted with his overeager assistant, Dana. Because ours was a tight-knit community—excluding me—I figured that meant he was too self-important to frequent our little diner.

That, or the rumormongers were right, and he really did spend all his time off realm saving lost souls and bringing them back here to start over. If the latter were true, then I had no use for him. I'd already lost one male hell-bent on being my savior, and I would never endure that loss again.

I rocked back, taking my feet with me. "Look, if you don't want to help make the payments, I'll take them out of my paycheck."

"It's not about the money." Emma slapped the empty mug from my hands. It collapsed in a spray of ceramic shards at my feet. "It's about you hiding out and living in denial, which isn't living at all. You speak more often to the day guard at Marchland Cemetery than you do the women and men living two houses down from us. You can't live among the dead."

I leaned forward, bracing my elbows on my knees. "I'm not your responsibility."

She captured my face between her palms. "I am bound to you by love, not obligation. You're the one trapped in the past, not me. It's time you start living or get on with dying." She stood, leaving her chair to rock angrily in her wake. "Either way, I'm washing my hands of you until you deal with this. I mean *really* deal with this."

She stalked over to the front door and slammed it solidly behind her, leaving the windowpanes to rattle like her teeth had in the cold.

Scattered beneath my rocker, the mug was past saving, but Emma's ultimatum made me wonder for the first time if maybe I wasn't.

Chapter Six

I rolled a couple of oranges across the countertop, sliced them in half, then settled them face down on the electric juicer. "Emma!" I stared at the ceiling overhead and yelled louder. "Breakfast is ready. Come and get it."

Over the grinding, whirring sounds of an orange dying, I heard the shrill ring of the telephone and grabbed it with juice-sticky fingers. "Hello?"

"Hello there, it's Dana, I just wanted to call and see how you were holding up this morning." A beat of silence passed. "Well? How are you?"

"Thanks for thinking of me. I'm feeling much better today." I smiled, thinking for the first time those words rang true. "Emma and I had a little talk, and I think I'm finally ready to lay Harper's memory to rest." I rescued bacon from the frying pan, using the spatula to drop the crisp strips onto a paper-towel-lined plate. Then I killed the flickering gas flame on the stove.

"I'm so glad to hear that." Dana's enthusiasm cranked up a few notches. "The fifth year marks the end..."

I tuned her out, listening to the floor creaking overhead accompanied by the dull thump of socked feet on the stairs. "Did you need to speak with Emma?"

Dana stopped talking mid-sentence. "I— Of course, that would be lovely."

Wouldn't it just? I snorted, covering the sound with a cough. Emma shuffled into the kitchen. Her wide-set eyes were still half closed with sleep and her unruly blonde curls flattened to one side of her head.

I pointed to the receiver tucked between my chin and shoulder. "Dana's on the phone."

Emma snatched the handset, pegging me with a bleary glare before addressing Dana. "Hmmph?"

I cut pats of butter and drizzled syrup over our waffles while Dana talked and Emma grunted in response. Then I set two places at the table and dropped into my chair in time to watch the three tries it took Emma to successfully hang the handset back in its cradle on the wall.

It fell, clattering onto the counter where we both ignored it. It was safer that way.

"What did Mary Sunshine want with you so bright and early?" I teased, mostly.

Emma glared through puffy eyes, stabbing a piece of waffle with more force than necessary and popping it into her mouth after missing the hole the first two tries. I pushed a mug of steaming black coffee towards her with the tip of my middle finger.

Her nostrils flared, eyes gone wild as her teeth bared in a low snarl. I glimpsed the old Emma in her expression, the one who would have stabbed someone with a crochet needle rather than knit them mittens. I flattened my hand on the tabletop, lowering my gaze from her eyes to her shoulder, submissive and uninterested, a posture I had perfected sometime between hitting puberty and Archer hitting me.

Emma's hand snapped forward as if magnetized, lunging for the handle and almost toppling her prize in the process. Fortunately, she ran more towards lethargic than lethal in the mornings. After she managed to stick her finger in the blistering liquid and added a few new words to the English language, I gave up and cupped her hands around the mug. Her first, audible swallow ended on a blissful sigh. She grunted again in acknowledgement, managing to sound more human.

Demon metabolism went haywire after consuming caffeine. It was addictive, not that Dana had bothered to impart that knowledge until after Emma had taken her first sip. I mean, humans thrived on the stuff, and Emma and I brewed more pots of coffee on any given day than we had pennies in the overflowing "take a penny" tray. We ran a diner after all. A word to the wise should have come standard.

According to Dana, again, after the fact, coffee became the over-the-counter drug of choice for the local demon youth within months of the colony's establishment. Unregulated, within easy reach, and completely harmless to humans, there wasn't much that could be done to curb the epidemic other than keep decaf on hand and learn to read the fine print on food labels.

Even some halflings suffered the metabolic woes of their half-demon heritage. Emma swore she didn't have a problem. Some mornings I wasn't so sure. Just to be on the safe side, I had slowly begun cutting Emma's morning brew with half-decaffeinated grounds. She pushed her mug away, frowning into its depths. I knew she'd figure it out sooner or later.

"It stopped snowing." I nibbled on a piece of bacon. "It's still pretty cloudy out there. I think we'll have rain moving in by the afternoon." I waited, watching her stab another waffle before checking my watch. "Are you going to shower before we head in to work?"

Emma upturned her mug, draining the last semi-caffeinated drops. "No work today." Her voice sounded rusty with disuse. "That's why Dana called. She wanted to tell us the town is still shut down from the snow yesterday." She picked over the remainder of her breakfast. "The inn is firing up its kitchen to feed the out-of-towners so we can have the day off." She pushed back from the table, carrying her dirty dishes as she went, effectively ending the conversation.

"This isn't about the weather, is it?" I carried my dishes over, bumped Emma out of the way with my hip and took her place at the sink. "I know we don't get much snow here, but the flurries yesterday are hardly reason enough to shut down the whole town." I peeked through the lace-lined windows into the backyard. "Most of it's melted already, so spill. What's going on?"

"We thought..." She cleared her throat. "*I* thought you might like the day to yourself." She pushed me aside to rinse her plate and cup in the sink. "I know you planned on going up to Marchland after work. This way you can be home around lunch."

I leaned over, propping my chin on her shoulder. "Thanks."

Emma patted my cheek with a damp hand. "You know, you could always stay home instead. I'm heading over to Dana's for the weekly women's circle meeting. All the wives will be there, even a few of the males hang out for a bit. It would give you a chance to mingle outside of taking their orders at the diner."

"Not today." I lost my chinrest when she moved away from me. "Maybe next week?"

Emma sighed, massaging her temples. "The time is coming where you're going to need their counsel. There are things you need to be told." She frowned. "You probably should have already been told."

"Soon," I promised, absently washing my dishes and setting them beside hers in the rack to dry.

"Not *soon*, tonight. The wives said you needed to know before." She sounded distant, uncertain. "But I thought you deserved to have at least one more day of peace."

I glanced at my sister. Shadows having nothing to do with the early hour darkened her eyes. She chewed her naked thumbnail, keeping her eyes downcast.

"Is something wrong?"

She waved away my worries. "It will keep a while longer."

We stood there for a minute or two with the hot-water pipes groaning in protest and the sink dripping into the basin.

"I'm taking your advice." I tried to sound casual. "When I go to Marchland...I'm saying my goodbyes to Harper."

Her hand dropped to her side. "Are you sure you don't want some company?"

"No, I'm good. I just need some time alone." A pent-up breath whistled through my lips. "You were right. I need to move on. I may not make it on the first try, but..." I shrugged, "...It's the best I can do."

Emma closed the distance between us and wrapped me in a hug that smelled of coffee and sister and hope. "I'm so proud of you. We'll make this work."

I sniffled through blurred vision.

She pulled back and caught my chin between her fingers. "You're going to make it. I promise." She gave a final tug, her voice filling with mischief. "Now that we have that settled, I've been thinking you might like a new companion. One who enjoys the outdoors almost as much as you? What about a pet?"

"*What about a pet?*" Excuses bubbled up, tripping out over my lips. "Animals don't like me. They bite, and claw, and look at me funny. It's not a good idea."

"You're being silly."

"You're half human. They like you." I stumbled backwards as if she could pull a puppy from her pocket. "I'm just, I don't know. I must smell like—something."

"You smell like something all right." Emma chuckled. "Like a hot date."

"I—" My jaw hung open, disbelieving. "What are you talking about?" I knew I didn't like being the center of their beady-eyed attention, but I'd been too busy extracting myself from their furry embraces to wonder why they acted that way. "The Moore's bull terriers..."

Emma continued to snicker. "They were humping your leg."

My cheeks flamed. Feeling my way along the counter, I palmed an orange left over from breakfast and hurled it right at her smirking face. It glanced off Emma's shoulder and rolled down the hall. I grabbed the phone next, but thought better of throwing it when I doubted my aim would be much improved. "I can't believe you didn't tell me." I groaned, covering my eyes with one hand. "No wonder everyone looks at me that way."

Emma's face split into a grin. "You're like one of those pet whisperers, only with a nine-hundred hotline voice."

"What is that supposed to mean?" Judging by her gasping breaths, it wasn't a good thing.

"A phone-sex operator." Emma's eyes rolled skyward. "You know, you call the number on television, get talked through a good time, and get charged out the wazoo for the privilege."

"No, I did *not* know." I dropped the cordless phone onto the counter, wiping my hand across my jeans but still managing to feel dirty. "How do you find out about this stuff?"

She sighed. "We've lived here for five years. I watch television, read books and keep my eyes open. I've even dated a couple of times, remember?"

I hadn't remembered. "Humans," I said, "from town."

Emma's lips hitched to one side. "Yes, the owner of the hardware store and the curly-haired realtor who blew through town a few months back." She laughed, but it was a tired sound. "Most of the demons are taken, and I'm half human anyway..." She scratched her fingernail across the countertop, picking at a spot of dried spaghetti sauce left over from the night before. "I loved Harper too, you know."

I tossed her a damp rag from the sink. "I know you did."

Instead of clearing, she glanced up at me, tilting her head to one side and pursing her lips. "Are you sure you don't want company?"

"I thought about asking you to go, but I think this is something I should do alone."

Emma nodded. "Yeah, okay. Just keep your cell phone turned on and in your pocket. If you need anything..."

I joined her on the braided rag rug, pulled her into my arms and squeezed. "I'll call you."

"You better. It's an hour there and an hour back. Three hours round trip *if you keep an eye on the time*." Her expression turned doubtful. "Just be home before nightfall."

I imagined her recalling all the times I'd become lost to my memories, burning away the daylight hours until I was forced to call her for a pickup. "I will."

She continued to frown. "I'm serious. You're as blind as a bat in the dark. Plus the rain." Emma's voice went stern. "Don't chance it."

I glanced over her head at the Felix the Cat clock mounted on the wall. "It's seven a.m. I have ten hours before dark, give or take a few. What's the worst that could happen?"

Chapter Seven

The front tires of my truck had rolled over the invisible line separating Cleburne and Randolph counties when a loud *pop* rang out over my right shoulder, followed by a steady *whomp, whomp, whomping.*

Slapping my open palms against the steering wheel, I guided the wobbling truck onto the hard shoulder of road. It coasted unsteadily to a stop in front of a green metal sign. "Welcome to Grove Oak" was the bold declaration. The city's singular attraction was spelled out in bold print one line lower, "Marchland Cemetery, Next Left."

I pushed open the door and stepped out onto slushy gravel. A few token drops of rain anointed my forehead and drew my eyes up to where blue-black storm clouds spilled across the sky like ink from a broken pen.

Glancing at the driver's-side tires, I frowned at them. Both were plump and taut. Rounding the tailgate to the passenger's side, I fought off the surge of annoyance tightening the muscles of my jaw. The rear rim sandwiched a mattress of deflated rubber, scored like a breakfast waffle, on thawing grass.

Kicking the sagging rubber blob, I was forced to consider my options. During our first year in the colony, Emma had forced me to complete the requisite courses to obtain our new citizenship. Including a driving school complete with vehicle operation and maintenance classes. So, I knew how to change a tire. In theory.

A muffled rumble of thunder deep in the angry sky forced a rapid choice. I decided I'd rather put my insurance premium to work by calling for roadside assistance. I slid my hand into the pocket of my jacket, groping for my phone that wasn't there.

"Hmmm." Frustration growing, I circled around to the open door and leaned across the bench seat until the piping cut into my stomach. Most of the time I left the backpack I used as a purse slumped on the floorboard and that's where it sat now. My fingers hooked the chestnut strap and hauled it up onto the seat where I dumped the bag's contents over the fake leather upholstery.

A miniature first-aid kit tumbled out followed by a nutrition bar, my billfold, a few feminine odds and ends, but no cellular phone.

A rush of air hissed through my teeth. This was not good. Impatiently, I crammed everything back into place. The hooked closure on the backpack snagged my sleeve, tumbling the bag onto the road and tipping its contents when I yanked my arm away. Items skittered across the pavement to lie still beneath the truck.

I had parked on an incline designed to guide rainwater into the ditches off to either side of the road. Bending down to retrieve my bits and not-so-valuable pieces, I lost my balance and braced my weight on the running board. Hinges groaned as the door swung closed, hitting my back in the gap where jeans and jacket didn't meet. I felt a searing stripe of pain where a deep line was scored across my spine.

"Un-freaking-believable." I stretched upwards to relieve the ache, taking the partially closed door in hand. Tensing my arm, I slammed it shut and rocked the truck with my irritation.

Suddenly, dread niggled at my senses. I pulled up on the door handle, but it refused to budge. I knew what I would see as I cupped my hands against the glass to peer inside. Yep. There they were. My keys dangled blatantly in the ignition.

Thump, thump, thump. My forehead hit on the glass several times. I spun around and collapsed against the truck, staring down the empty road. Bleak old-growth oak trees strung with moss lined both sides of the pavement. Flickering shadows prowled beneath the canopy of leaves. Automatically, I rubbed my arms to quell those prickles riding my skin in the rising chill. There was no way I wanted to be trapped out here alone. So much death, even peaceful death, was eerie.

I felt insane for driving out to pay homage to a blank marker and the barren grave. Emma had insisted this empty symbol would give me a sense of closure. Harper's funeral rites had been performed there too, but I'd forbidden the colony to add his name to the marble. To see it etched in stone would have broken me in the early days. Even now, I wasn't too keen on the idea.

Screened behind the grove of trees, a black wrought-iron fence ran the length of the road and towered over the sloped banks dropping into the deeper of the two drainage ditches. The guard shack sat at the edge of my vision, welcoming visitors to the cemetery.

Scooping the last of my belongings off the pavement under the truck, I slung the bag over my shoulder. Taking a deep breath of cold air, I moved towards the lights. Soggy gravel crunched at every step of my tennis shoes. I had only covered half the distance down the lane when the bottom of the threatening storm fell out.

Wind whipped at my skin as it drove solid pellets of rain in stinging slaps on my neck and face. Thunder crashed as lightning brushed veined fingers across the sky. The dim glow of light called to me from a few hundred yards ahead. I ran, slipping and sliding over ground undecided whether it wanted to refreeze or melt.

The toe of my right sneaker touched on a patch of ice and sent me skating the last few feet until my outstretched hands smacked into the thin metal wall of the guard shack. Through the window centered in the door, I saw Jacob Mathews sitting at his desk, newspaper in hand, staring back at me. I gave a weak wiggle of my stinging fingers as he came over to investigate.

"Madelyn." He greeted me warmly, stepping aside to allow me to enter. "Nasty day for paying visits."

"Hey, Jacob." I skirted around his body while he partially blocked the door. "It's just tradition, I guess. I always drive up the day after." My shoulder brushed against his chest, and he sucked in a harsh breath. "Are you okay?"

He rubbed the spot and grinned. "I'm about to be."

I returned the smile, uncomfortable, but uncertain how much to blame on my lack of social graces versus any intentions he might have had for making me feel that way.

Jacob's khaki uniform strained over a thickly muscled chest, leading to a tapered waist that put mine to shame. I tried not to stare, but the proportions weren't quite right for either a man or a male of his species. He seemed to have trouble holding his glamour, and I didn't like what I saw through the illusion. Too late, I wished I'd stayed at the truck in the rain instead of seeking shelter here.

I glanced down at the water pooling at my feet, desperate for any distraction. "Sorry about the mess. Do you have a mop or something?"

He turned away, taking the two steps needed to reach a

small card table holding a coffeepot and a stack of a Styrofoam cups. "I've been expecting you."

I pasted on my best service-with-a-smile grin. "Well, here I am. Now, about that mop?"

He poured himself a cup of sludge that could tentatively be labeled as coffee. The consistency was wrong, thick and syrupy instead of thin and liquid. His gaze met mine and the very corner of his eye twitched. "This year makes five years." He took a sip then stepped forward, tracking me.

Fear skittered along my spine. Dana had mentioned the fifth year too. They both made the word sound less like a number and more like a deadline. One I'd passed. "Yes, it does."

His eyes flashed all black, a demon's black. "The time for mourning Harper has passed." His large body crowded mine as his gaze traveled languidly over me, snagging at the level of my breasts. "I've waited for this day." His tongue swiped across his lower lip. "For you."

My heart thundered in my ears, drowning out the staccato beat of rain on the tin roof. Cold sweat beaded at the base of my spine, mingled with rain, and rolled lower. "What are you talking about?" I shoved against the solid wall of Jacob's chest, but he didn't budge.

His low chuckle reverberated throughout the booth. "You don't remember me, do you, *princess*?"

"What is your problem?" My breaths came quicker, and the nubbins just behind my shoulders tensed, preparing for a flight to safety I could never make.

"I was a slave in your house. For years I watched you call Harper to your chambers at night while the rest of us fought for bedding or slept on the cold stone floor." His hand lifted, revealing clawed tips on the ends of each finger. "Your protection as his chosen expires today. It's been five years since he failed to return to you, and your sweet..." he leaned over, inhaling deeply, "...sweet flesh is mine for the claiming."

I flattened against the door, reaching one hand behind my back to grope blindly for the doorknob. "No, it wasn't like that."

His pupils flashed silver. "Then tell me what it was like!" His fist punched through the wall beside my head, crumpling the corrugated panel like a well-placed foot on a soda can. "Did he love you? Truly love you? Or were you only a warm bed and willing body for him?"

"He loved me." Harper's admission had been the last words he'd spoken to me. Even in the midst of half-truths and whole lies, I believed he'd meant them. I had to.

"You sound uncertain, highness."

Jacob stroked hot fingers down my cheek. Blood pearled where sharp claws met soft skin. "Your scent is maddening." He lifted damp hair smelling of an herbal shampoo I would never use again and sniffed. "Did you know that?" His tongue lapped away the crimson droplets staining my cheek. "Mmm." His chest rumbled under my palm.

"Stop it." Fear made my voice waver, and judging by his grin, he'd noticed too.

"I don't think so. I heard the women talking after you first arrived. You had no idea that Harper had been to this realm, let alone aided in the creation of the colony." His eyes were vacant pools of malevolence. "Have you searched for his face among the children?" Jacob laughed darkly. "Did you find it?"

My mind screamed in instant denial even as it flipped through a rolodex of youthful faces living within the colony that fit the right age and appearance. I shut down those thoughts hard. "I came to pay my respects, not to be intimidated." The backpack slipped from my shoulder until the strap dangled from my open hand. "I'm leaving now."

"No." He nestled his face in the crook of my neck. "I'm afraid I can't let you do that."

"Don't do this." I tensed and tightened my grip on the strap. He must have felt it because his hand traveled down my arm to snatch the satchel from my grasp and toss it to the floor behind us.

He'd taken my only weapon. No matter that it was no match for thick Evanti hide, I'd felt safer having that tiny assurance in my hand, and he'd ripped it away, leaving me with no option but to bluff my way out of this mess. "I'm under the colony leader's protection. Clayton won't let this go unpunished. You're a fool to even consider it."

"Then I'm a fool." Jacob groaned against my neck, nipping his way across my collarbone. One wrong move from me and he could tear my throat out so quickly I would have a moment or two before realizing I was already dead. "All the unmated Evanti will come for you. You may be a half breed, but you're the only unmated female of our kind in the colony. You've never seen the frenzy, the fight for a female's favor. Blood will flow." His teeth captured skin between them, reinforcing my earlier imaginings. "You could save lives by agreeing to be mine."

"You're crazy."

His large palm wrapped around the front of my throat. "I am what your mother made me," he enunciated slowly, fingers tightening.

I tried to pry away his hands, but failed. His breath carried the scent of stale coffee from what must have been hours spent sipping and waiting for my arrival. Why else would the trashcan be overflowing with crushed cups and the burned dregs of distilled caffeine left bubbling in the pot on the burner? The high flooding his system would override his basic decency, if he had any left.

"I'm sorry for what she did to you."

"Not yet, you're not." His tongue delved inside my ear. "But you will be."

I believed him. The sterling shine in his eyes kicked my instincts in gear as fight-or-flight adrenaline surged through me. Years of squaring off with Emma had primed my body for this eventuality and I was ready.

Smoothing my hands up Jacob's biceps, I rested them on his shoulders. He groaned his approval, squeezing harder, cutting off my air supply. I braced against him, regaining my balance, and then brought my knee up between his thighs hard enough to rattle his teeth. He pulled back, eyes wide and losing their focus. His fingers flexed open, releasing me as he cupped his groin with one hand and braced against the wall with the other.

The doorknob spun in my hand, opening the door on the storm as wind and rain raced inside the small building and whipped around us, blowing hair into my eyes.

Jacob glanced up, panting. "Do it." He bared stark, white teeth. "Run. I like to chase." He twisted to brace his forearm against the wall, resting his face in the bend of his elbow and hiding his eyes. "I'll even give you a head start."

I backed out the door and slammed it firmly shut between us for all the good it would do me. I watched through the window in helpless fascination as his glamour fell away. Light skin became dark. Wings seemed to burst from his back as the appearance of humanity melted away to reveal his true form.

The part of me likened to him wanted to stay and touch those red wings fluttering provocatively, luring me past caution. "It's a mating dance," I said, swallowing a sour lump in my throat, knowing what would happen if I stepped back across the threshold. Still I allowed the rhythmic flitter to lull me and make me want on such a primal level I couldn't break the enthrallment.

His soft laughter cut through the thin metal panel separating us. "So you're not immune." He flicked his bright, fleshy wings. "Good to know."

My mouth watered. The doorknob, half twisted, filled my palm. I stared at my hand, moving independently of thought and working to get me closer to what my body craved. Something was wrong with me, and Jacob, but I didn't know what, and it was too late to ask now.

Emma had known. How could she not have warned me? This, whatever it was, must have been the cause of her apprehension this morning. My jaw tightened. Dana had known it too. I had been the one left unaware of my circumstances and, if Jacob caught me, I would be the one to pay.

I pried my fingers free, watching the release of each individual digit. Once my eye contact broke away from the sensuous display inside the building, I could think again. I turned around and surveyed my surroundings. To my left sat the open road and my useless truck. To my right, white marble headstones dappled the hillside. *Damn it.* I had to choose and fast.

Jacob's singsong voice cut through the chaos of my thoughts. "Ready or not, here I come."

I didn't make a conscious decision. My legs started pumping, eating up the ground between the guard shack and the graveyard. Debris exploded outward as the door I'd closed on Jacob hurled by my ear and embedded in the base of an oak tree to my left. I raised my forearm, blocking my eyes from the showered splinters of impact.

Behind me, I heard the snap of wings unfurling. A breeze kicked up, fanned by what had to be Jacob's launch skyward.

My legs pumped harder but were no match for a male demon in his prime.

"Mad-el-yn," he called, swooping closer. "Run little demoness. Make me work for my reward." His talon-tipped fingers brushed through my hair, snagging in the damp length. Hot breath lifted the fine hairs on the back of my neck with rising fear.

In my peripheral vision, I saw Jacob gliding effortlessly beside me. I had to do something or else he'd keep pace until my legs gave out and then take me where I fell. Princess Madelyn DeGray had been raised to be a victim, but the waitress Maddie Toliver was not going down without a fight. I just needed a way to level the playing field.

Changing direction, I veered abruptly towards the oak grove, leaping over fallen logs as I ran for the shelter of the forest. The low-lying branches would render his wings useless, but earned me only a slight advantage because demons were fast and pissed-off demons were nearly impossible to outmaneuver. As I ran, tree limbs slapped my face and roots hooked my feet as if trying to slow me down and hold me captive for him. Each delay cost me seconds I didn't have to spare.

"Come out, little princess." Somewhere behind me wood snapped on a harsh growl. *"Princess?"*

My feet alternately bogged in mud and slipped on ice patches, making me curse this climate for luring demons down south in the first place. I ran full out until my legs wobbled and caved beneath me, dropping me all too soon on my butt. The muscles in my legs jiggled like Jell-O, but I knew Jacob was close and I had to move.

A copper flash out of the corner of my eye brought my head around to a fallen oak tree where a pair of citrine eyes peered out at me. They blinked once and vanished, much to my relief. Despite Emma's assurances, I didn't want to take my chances with the local wildlife.

Pushing to my knees, I got my feet under me, still shaky but doable. I'd wasted the precious few minutes of lead time I'd gained by taking this route. Now I had to make a decision and time was running out. I glanced over and the animal, a fox, darted from its den, trotted a quick circle around my legs and went back inside. I looked at it and it at me, neither of us quite sure what to make of the other. The fox stepped back out, made a show of turning, and went back inside the den.

Zaniah help me, I took its invitation, well aware I was too large for the meager shelter it offered to share. I walked until the end of my shoes disappeared inside the hole and then dropped to my hands and knees. Hope flared white hot and burned through my exhaustion when I realized what I'd found.

Built beneath the fallen oak was an opening almost two feet squared, kept hidden by shadow and mounded leaves. But what made up my mind was the thin veil of glamour cast over the entrance. Evanti could shroud their bodies, but not physical locations. Something else had created this haven with a gentle touch that seemed to pulse with welcoming vibrations.

Mindful of my host, I lowered my legs inside and wiggled down until the ground swallowed me whole. Inside the burrow, I had a foot of clearance above my head and a few feet of space stretching out on either side. Clearly, not an animal's home, but what else could it be?

The fox wove through my cramped legs, pausing to rub against my hand like a cat.

"You'll be safe here."

"You talked," I said on a harsh whisper, plastering myself against the dirt wall as far away as I could get. I must have hit my head when I fell. Only I didn't remember falling. I'd crawled in under my own power.

Grasping for any anchor in reality, I allowed roots to tangle in my fingers, surprising me by how real this hallucination felt. I glanced down at the small animal who absolutely had not spoken to me. "You're not real."

"As you will." Its dainty, furred shoulder rolled in careless dismissal. *"Stay here and I will fetch Clayton."*

"How do you know—?"

"Shhh, the other will find you if you can't keep quiet." The fox, a vixen from the sound of her voice, which I absolutely did not hear inside my head, walked to the small opening.

"I—"

"Shhh." She glanced over her shoulder, warning me again with a snap of her jaws.

My head jerked up and down in a shaky nod. With a flick of her plush red tail the fox slipped out, kicking more leaves over the entrance with her nimble hind legs before sprinting away into the dark maw of the forest. I wanted to call the apparition back. But she had vanished in a blur of russet fur, assuming she *was* real and not a product of my desperate imagination.

The scent of damp earth and wet, rotting leaves swamped my sense of smell where I rested my head against the dirt wall. I adjusted my legs and slid down into a more comfortable position. Alone and afraid, I tried to reassure myself. *I am not crazy.* The mantra soothed me, so I added a few more things to the list.

Foxes cannot talk. I am not in a burrow underground hiding from a coffee-addicted, would-be rapist. I must have slipped getting into the truck when I left the house this morning. I'm probably lying on my back in a patch of ice in front of the house. When Emma gets home, we'll laugh about it and...

Then I heard it—that stillness that comes with the absence of sound. Outside of my hidey-hole, silence reigned. No pitter-patter of falling rain. No birdsong, no wind or trees creaking—just absolute, utter quiet.

A twig snapped, echoing sharply amid so much stillness. I flinched when Jacob called out to me. "You've hidden." His voice rose. "I'm disappointed. I had hoped to catch you, mark your body among the tombs as we lay your ghost to rest. Now you've forced me to take you where I find you." He paused. "And I will find you."

A dull thump sounded overhead as pieces of decayed wood sifted down and into my hair. He stood on the log directly over me. I prayed the old wood would hold and his weight wouldn't send him crashing through the rotted tree trunk to land on top of me.

I didn't dare to breathe. Dust tickled my nose, tempting me to sneeze, so I cupped a hand over my face. I closed my eyes, picturing myself back home rocking with Emma on our rundown porch while picking paint chips for the grand renovation she had planned.

Above me the log groaned and more dust sprinkled my clothes. I heard a heavy thud as Jacob's feet hit the ground after leaping from his perch on the log. The den went dark as black ankles blocked the meager light from filtering through to where I sat. Red talons protruded from his heels, tapping idly on the ground while piercing through leaves and mulch on the forest floor.

Fear tied my stomach neatly into knots. Suddenly, letting an enraged and aroused demon find me in a burrow big enough for two didn't seem like such a great idea. I cursed the damn fox for leading me into what could become my final resting place and me for being fool enough to follow her. What had I been thinking? Oh yeah, that I didn't want Jacob to find me out in the open, either.

He turned so his toes pointed directly towards me, almost at the level of my eyes. I waited, expecting his foot to test the opening or him to drop onto his stomach and explore the entrance just large enough for a frightened demoness to slip inside to seek refuge.

My hands trembled where they rested on my knees. I shoved them between my thighs and clamped my legs together until the nervous twitching stopped.

Outside, thunder clapped and rain began again.

"Madelyn," said Jacob. "I will find you. And laws or no laws, no one will keep me from you." Then he roared, "You are mine!"

My ears rang from the ferocity of his cry, the sound so filled with hate and twisted with desire that it sickened me, terrified me to the marrow of my bones because I knew he believed it.

I saw muscle shift as Jacob's Achilles tendon flexed and his toes dug into the ground while rolling onto the balls of his feet. I heard the snap of leather pulling taut, a muttered curse, and then he was gone.

I could no longer feel my fingers so I loosened my thighs and let my hands quiver fitfully on the tops of my legs. My lungs expanded fully for the first time since entering the guard shack and released a foggy breath that was full of gratefulness to be alive. The bone-biting cold went unnoticed by me as I evaluated my position.

After living a half-life for so long, I had thought myself ambivalent to its continuance, but when faced with death, I had been afraid. I didn't want to die. I needed to curse flat tires and run through rain, sand old paint and put up wallpaper, bicker with Emma over silly unimportant things, come and go as I pleased, see...

I wanted to live. It was as simple as that.

The corner of my lips kicked up in a grin. Too bad it had taken a face-off with a demon, a figment of my own imagination and the promise of hours trapped underground to convince me life really was worth living.

Chapter Eight

Shivering, I kept track of time by the faint glow of my Timex wristwatch. Sometime between the start of rippling cramps from a missed lunch and the gradual fade to black of my vision, I decided Figment, the name I had given the fox, had stood me up. Night had fallen and I had to move.

I doubted the cavalry was on its way or it would have been here by now. Figment either didn't exist—and I had been crazy to believe a wild animal could somehow bring help—or she did exist and I was...well...slightly less crazy but still trapped with no help looming on the horizon. Not that I would see them at this point. Only the sensation of movement told me when I waved my hand in front of my face. Darkness rendered my eyes totally useless in distinguishing my surroundings.

Gnawing hunger and the pressure of need to use a restroom gave me two options. I could either stay put and hope Figment returned with Clayton—which seemed far-fetched even inside my own mind—or I could crawl out and then make a run for it in the hope I reached town before Jacob could mark me as his. He could be patiently sitting outside waiting to pounce as soon as I left the safety of this burrow. That notion caused the tip of my tongue to flick out and moisten my cracked, dry lips as I swallowed the thought.

Blood pumped and swelled painfully through my muscles

as I inched my way forward to the reality of the world outside. My joints protested the long, enforced stasis as I coaxed my knees to bend under me. Lifting my head slowly above ground level, I watched as pale, shimmering light reflected on the rain-kissed forest floor to illuminate what normally was invisible in the dark. It was just enough of a glimmer to let my sight adjust to cautiously scan the immediate area around the mouth of the burrow.

The fresh odor of wet leaves and the sharp essence of pine tangled as I inhaled deeply of the world beyond my hidey-hole. Every scent carried a welcome nuance of enticing escape. The hours of smelling damp earth seared a metallic tang on my tongue. Dust had sifted to the back of my throat, drier than a summer wind over Rihos.

I needed to cough, badly, but fear of discovery smothered the impulse. Instead, I took short, silent breaths. Clean, crisp-cold air shifted the dust deeper into my lungs. The forest floor rolled like a sea of darkness. The steady drizzle of rain had melted away the remnants of snow patches that could have helped me to safely navigate the indistinguishable murky ground lost in the night shadows.

I was a field mouse, quivering in the knowledge danger lurked out there and debating whether it was worth risking the deadly bite of the owl's razor claws to scamper out into the open. Here I was safe and hidden. At least for now.

To venture out could mean death striking on vibrant, crimson wings. It would not be a quick, merciful end, but a slow meting out of punishments until Jacob felt the scales were balanced between Mother and him or I died in the process. Whatever his plans, they did not bode well for me.

I had to get out and away from here, and far away from Jacob. Raising my head higher, I tried to suppress a deep sense of foreboding. Still it coursed through me as if I were preparing to have Madame Guillotine's blade slice through my spinal cord, separating life from body as my head rolled loosely away. The macabre image blinded me to the forest momentarily.

I waited, listening, seeking in the gloom a movement in the depths. When Jacob failed to jump out and yell "gotcha", confidence drew me to wiggle out on my stomach until I cleared the hole. Pushing to my feet, I took a few halting steps in a direction where I felt the cemetery's fence line ran, obscured by trees and the night. My legs wobbled as I stumbled forward. Cold numbed the protest of inactive muscles pushed into vigorous action. I made a bush my forest restroom.

The cold nipped at my bared skin. I quickly got on with it, ready to pull my jeans up fast. It wouldn't be funny to be literally caught out in the open with my pants down and a randy demon seizing the opportunity to wreak his promised vengeance. That potential threat made me hike them up roughly. My fingers tingled with pins and needles as I fumbled the zipper and studs of my jeans.

No bogeyman pounced on me. Nothing swooped from the canopy overhead to tear me from the ground screaming into the night. Air rushed jerkily out of me as I smoothed the cough that had waited patiently to erupt and dispel the dusty accumulation. My clammy palms glided on the rough denim of my torn blue jeans. I knew better than to hope Jacob had given up the chase. It would take more than the scarce hours I'd spent underground to evaporate the kind of hatred for me reflected in his frenzied eyes.

Instinct and memory kicked in to guide me over the uneven terrain. Everything merged and melded together. I couldn't tell up from down on the rough surface tearing at my frozen feet. Solid ground squelching beneath my soles and the weightlessness of air surrounding me reassured my senses of where and how my unwilling limbs moved.

A root caught my toe. Tripping, I fell to my knees, jarring my elbows as they took the brunt of my forward fall. Catching my breath, I hauled myself back up. Stumbling on, I came to a sharp stop. Black lines scored my vision. Grimy fingers rubbed my eyes. Were they real? I blinked. The vertical bars were still there, unmoving. Stretching a hand in front of me, frigid steel bruised my knuckles. The cemetery fence. I'd made it. What next? I was too exhausted to think clearly.

Lacing my fingers through the bars, I pressed my forehead against them. If I strained my eyes, I could just make out the straight ribbon of asphalt below that offered salvation into town. Walking along the road would be the fastest and simplest way to get there. And the most likely route to attract unwanted attention.

A hazy twinkle rose just above the surface of the road, far enough away it took a few minutes to expand and separate into twin orbs of light. Hitchhiking at this hour from this place held little appeal. But the idea of being found face down in the cemetery garnered even less. Raising my arm, I allowed the shadow of my hand to shield my sight against the glare of vehicle lights on high beam. It was now or never. I had to make my move.

Rain-slicked steel slipped through my grip as I hauled my weight upwards and over. The spear tips snagged my jacket, throwing me off balance as I dropped into a crouch on the other side. Those headlights appeared higher than I had first thought and closer than I had realized. The driver was seriously speeding.

Desperately, I skidded down the sharp embankment to land with a sloppy splash in the stream of icy rainwater running through the bottom of the roadside drainage ditch.

Clay oozed between my grasping fingers as I sought secure anchorage by using dead weeds to clamber out. Mud sucked at my feet as I pulled free of the water.

I stumbled onto the blacktop, my arms waving madly like a windmill in the oncoming traffic lane. Light washed over me, blinding me to the vehicle's speed and location. I didn't waste precious breath calling out. There was little chance the driver would hear me anyway. I stood a better chance at broadcasting my location to Jacob than soliciting help.

The lights dipped as the driver braked and screeched to an uncomfortably close stop. I kept waving as I half ran, half tripped across the double lines to reach the stationary vehicle. The whir of a window lowering and the cough of a voice clearing pinpointed the driver's location. Those blazing headlights burned away any semblance of vision I needed to see who my savior was.

A feeble voice called through the open window. "Did you lose your way?"

"Yes, sir, I did." Relief swamped me, excising my initial hesitation. "My truck broke down and this crazy man chased me into the woods. I need to get into town and call my sister. Is there any way you can give me a lift?"

"Of course I can." Sincerity crackled in his assurance.

"Oh, thank you so much." My feet moved me towards him. Out of the glare of the headlights my eyes refocused, adjusting to the lack of light. My knees threatened to give way under me as the blue cab of my Ford F150 materialized in front of me.

"You're very welcome." The frail edge left his voice as the driver's side door swung open. "*Princess.*" Black combat boots capped by bloused khaki pants impacted the pavement with an ominous thud.

My tongue turned to sand as I mouthed the one name I

dreaded. "Jacob."

I didn't see him move. One minute I stood frozen, a hapless deer caught in his headlights. The next, a freight train constructed of unyielding demon flesh slammed into me, lifting me from the pavement and rolling with me onto the shoulder of the road. Scalding heat burned my knees and elbows where the abrasive asphalt scrubbed flesh from bone.

We rolled and slid down the clay-slick walls of the drainage ditch in a knot of struggling limbs. His massive body rolled atop mine. I tried to bring my knee up between his thighs, but he had learned his lesson that first time. Catching my ankle, he braced a hand on my leg and twisted. A sickening pop filled the air. Sharp pinpoints of pain radiated in my knee and shin where bone and tendons no longer connected.

"Now, now," Jacob grunted, shoving open my thighs and settling between them. "Play nice and we'll get along just fine."

"Fuck you!" My fingernails plowed angry furrows into his skin. Jacob's flesh peeled away beneath my fingertips.

His bellow of rage pounded my eardrums to the point they buzzed with the sound of nothing, leaving me momentarily deaf. Jacob hoisted me up by my shirtfront before flipping me and forcibly smashing me face down into the freezing stream swirling through the bottom of the ditch. Water swamped my face, flushing up my nose as I sucked it into my mouth in a futile attempt to scream.

His large, coarse fingers clenched my hair in a vicious grip as he shoved my head deeper into the muddy water. Fire raged in my lungs as I desperately fought to keep from inhaling fluid. I coughed and struggled, but only managed to gulp down more rainwater. Without the use of my left leg, and trapped beneath the large male's body, I had no leverage to launch a counterattack. There was nothing to do but drown.

I inhaled water. Without oxygen, I was dying, but I was damned if I would go without a fight. Twisting and thrashing, I tried to break Jacob's deadly grip. Long minutes dragged on, perhaps only mere seconds. The rising pulse of my straining heart tattooed out the number of beats and seconds passing. Time became meaningless.

My body relaxed, growing limp. A sense of weightlessness tugged at my consciousness to let go. One hand kept my head under while the fingers of Jacob's other hand crushed my windpipe, breaking the avenue for my last gasp. He kept up the pressure until breath became a distant memory and suffocation a promise I longed to see fulfilled.

One final violent convulsion and I twisted my head sideways under the water. Through the distortion of the stream I saw Jacob's pupils flash silver. His head snapped to the side. My ears were plugged with sludge, but I felt the vibrations of speech through the hands holding me under. He couldn't see my smile at the sweet relief awaiting me on the other side of so much loss.

At least in death, pain could no longer plague me. Memories would no longer assail me. I would be free. I accepted my fate, embraced where circumstance had led me, and said a silent goodbye to my sister.

Oh, Emma, how I'll miss you...

Then Jacob's weight was gone. I floated in the water, too weak to raise my head to save myself. Heavy hands clutched my shoulders, lifting me from the murk and mud. My open eyes were unseeing. My heart had stilled. I was leaving and did not need to return. Being shaken like a rag doll failed to raise a response from my limp body.

Warm lips covered mine as I lay on my back in the cold of the night. Air was forced into me before a fist pounded my chest. The power of that impact jump-started my heart. Blood ripped through my arteries to feed a starving brain. Paralyzed lungs convulsed to thrust a jet of water through clenched teeth and soaked my face, my chin, my hair, my shirt. The flow felt warm against the ice of my skin.

"Maddie!" Someone called my name. I didn't know who, or why the voice sounded so familiar.

My head lolled sharply to the side. I had no strength to lift it.

Velvety soft, melodic and intimate, the deep tones gently caressed my senses. "Hold on, I'm going to get you out of here."

The sweet ache of recognition filled me. "Harper?" I struggled to grasp the root of that sound, to hold something once lost to me in my hands and celebrate it being found.

The voice dipped to a disappointed sigh. "No, I'm Clayton Delaney."

Awareness flared in the farthest corner of my mind. So this was my generous benefactor come to save me. In the ditch there was no light to show me his face. Not that it would have helped much.

I had no impression of wings, but in this realm, most Evanti maintained their human glamour and their privacy. What I did sense was power. Raw and very male. Energy vibrated in the air between us.

"Oh." More slime from my lungs choked me as the silt clogged the back of my throat. I had begun to think Clayton Delaney was a pseudonym for Dana Evans since I'd never seen or spoken to him but she was always *fresh from a meeting* with the mysterious colony leader. But he felt real enough to me now.

His wet shirt hugged a hard body. My hands rested on his waist, his on my shoulders. His heat radiated through the damp fabric into my palms, heating me to my core. "Jacob—"

"Is being dealt with in accordance with the laws of the colony." Clayton's thumbs worked over my shoulder so lightly I wondered if he even realized what he was doing. The touch was affectionate, soothing, and I wanted to blame the connection I felt on his voice, but couldn't. There was much more to this male than anyone had let on. Of that I was certain.

"Your sister shouldn't have allowed you to come alone today." His soft touch hardened. "She nearly cost you your life."

I bristled, hackles lifting as I rose to her defense. Although I'd harbored similar thoughts myself, this was between Emma and I to resolve. He had no stake in the matter.

"Emma was allowing me time to grieve."

"Time you didn't have." His teeth snapped closed. His sweet breath filled my water-logged lungs. "I'm going to lift you. Just hold on to me."

I obeyed as Clayton scooped an arm beneath the bend of my knees. The broken leg bent at an odd angle. "What did he do to you?" He brushed a hand down my thigh, leaving a tingling trail in its wake. His fingers whispered over broken bone and shredded flesh. "He will pay for this, *deshiel.*"

I frowned at his use of the unexpected endearment until his other arm wrapped around my back, resting just below my shoulder blades. His fingers hesitated as they smoothed over the bumps he found there. He swore under his breath, jerking his hand farther down my back before lifting me up.

Heat flushed my cheeks. Harper had overlooked my physical imperfections. It hurt that this near-stranger couldn't. Shame cut away the worst of my disorientation. Clayton's disgust with my deformity pricked my pride for reasons I didn't want to examine too closely.

He cradled me against his chest, tucking his chin over the

crown of my head. I felt the ripple of his muscles as they tensed, then the rush of air—a tantalizing taste of flight—as he used his wings, suddenly in evidence, to lift us from the gutter and back onto the level pavement.

Clayton carried me around to the passenger side of my truck, shifting me gently until he managed to open the door and settle me on the bench seat. The interior light cast a soft glow around me, revealing filthy jeans and soggy shoes. And blood, lots of blood. It couldn't all be mine, could it?

I flinched when I caught the gleam of metal reflecting in Clayton's hand. His face was cast in shadow, and he seemed content to stay there. Across his palm, he revealed a small pocketknife. "I need to cut the fabric away from the wound so I can see what we're dealing with."

With one clean swipe, he cleaved the denim of my jeans leg in two, revealing the worst of the already-healing wounds. "The bone pierced through your skin." He bent down to examine the break. His head lowered, exposing slicked-back ebony hair curling just below his ears. No wonder he blended so well into the night. The color was natural, although the cut might not be. His glamour was a low hum moving over my skin everywhere his fingers touched.

Clayton's silence drew my attention. I coughed to clear my sore throat and tried to assure him. "I'll be fine, really."

"You're hardly bleeding." He sounded confused by the lack of flowing blood, but I didn't feel like explaining my whacked-out physiology just then. He cupped my ankle in hand and helped me pivot until my knees faced forward and my back flexed comfortably into the seat. "Good girl. Just sit tight and I'll get you home."

Clayton leaned over me, putting us chest to chest as he fastened my seat belt. He glanced up and I saw his face fully for the first time. My tortured heart rate skyrocketed. The air seemed to thin until the lack of oxygen made my head swim. I couldn't stop the accusation from rolling off my tongue.

"You look just like him."

The unspoken name hung in the air. Clayton's shuttered expression told me he knew exactly who I meant.

"I should." He pulled back, holding the door wedged open. His face remerged with the shadows. "Harper was my brother."

My jaw dropped as the door slammed shut on the dozens of questions scalding the tip of my tongue. I needed to ask, to seek reassurance he spoke the truth. He prowled around the front of my truck to speak with two males in full glamour I hadn't noticed. Through the wall of bodies, I saw Jacob held limply between them. Clayton patted the nearest male on the shoulder, hooked his thumb towards me and then pointed down the road behind me.

He glanced up and our eyes met through the windshield. His were such a curious mix of blue gray. I found myself wishing I could look beneath to discover if the black of his eyes was as conflicted as the illusion he cast over them. He continued talking to the others while keeping his gaze locked to mine. Waving them off, he started towards the door left open by Jacob's hasty exit.

The door closed and sealed us in an intimate bubble. I couldn't let the chance pass. I had to ask. "Why didn't anyone tell me?" For five years I had lived a stone's throw away from someone of Harper's bloodline. Someone I would have welcomed as family during those bleakest times of my life, someone who apparently didn't feel the same way about me.

Clayton ran a hand through his hair, pushing the damp tangle from his eyes. "Dana spoke with your sister after Harper failed to return home." He carefully skirted the issue of death.

"My brother resembled me, as you've noticed. They decided I should stay away and allow you to mourn without the visual reminder that your lover hadn't returned."

"He wasn't my lover." The words rushed out until I clamped a hand over my lips. I don't know why I said it. My heart ached the second I refuted the claim.

Clayton's voice lowered to a husky growl. "I don't want details."

"Oh." Blood rushed to my cheeks. "Of course you don't. I didn't mean— I just— Sorry."

His long fingers circled the gear shift. "Don't worry about it." He threw the truck into drive, and as he executed a three-point turn, the headlights washed over the demons dragging their quarry farther into the night.

I knew Clayton wanted silence. I could sense it in the tight clench of his jaw and tense hold on the wheel, but I wanted to know. "Why didn't Harper tell me he had a brother?" I paused, hearing nothing but the steady hum of the motor.

For a moment, he sat silently, ignoring me. His fingers flexed a little as if only now realizing how tight his grip had been. "I didn't know my brother," he corrected, "didn't know I had a brother until the day my father assigned me to border patrol."

"Border patrol?"

"I am freeborn." He grinned with pride and my heart raced in response. "I've never known Askaran *hospitality*."

His joke fell short because I knew what I was, what my mother had been and still was, and he did too. He glanced over and caught me picking my fingernails to avoid his assessment. "I apologize. You aren't responsible for your mother's actions. The Askaran society is cancerous. I'm glad you escaped." He didn't say *before you were tainted*, but I heard the words as

99

clearly as if he had spoken them.

"It's all right. I was raised apart from my family. I didn't realize how bad things were until shortly before...before we left." And when I'd found out, I had been horrified. Slavery had only been the tip of the iceberg, with worse things hidden just below the surface. Abuse, neglect, rape, all things centered on the Askaran craving for the depraved.

"I know. I saw you once, a very long time ago." Dimples winked in Clayton's cheeks as though he were remembering something amusing.

"What were you thinking just now?"

"I was remembering the first time I saw you." His cheek smoothed. Instead, he seemed contemplative as he recalled the memory for us both. "I served under my father in the freeborn legion. When my turn for patrol came up on the roster, I did something I normally wouldn't have done. I flew through Rihos, over the courtyard of the summer castle, and saw an angel and a demon playing together in the gardens. You couldn't have been more than ten or eleven years old." He frowned. "I knew the boy was blood kin. His wings carried the same crosshatch pattern all those of our line bear. But you..." he glanced my way, then resumed his stare, "...were enchanting."

I admired his profile using the pale illumination of the speedometer. From this angle, he looked less familiar. His face seemed more rounded and less angular than Harper's had been. "Why do you say that?"

This time Clayton didn't answer. He kept his eyes on the road and drove. I leaned my head back against the seat and closed my eyes, rocking over the uneven surface and fighting the call of sleep. I think I dozed off because all too soon I heard the rhythmic click of the turn signal, then the nose of the truck dipped in a pothole. I was home.

I opened my eyes to the familiar outline of the farmhouse I shared with Emma. Every light burned bright and every window's curtain was parted. Clayton parked beside Emma's matching truck, and then slid off the seat and into the night.

My door opened with a suctioned pop. I saw him hesitate. A fresh wave of humiliation flooded me. I imagined him remembering the feel of those bony stubs. They represented a death sentence to the Evanti. Flight was soul food their hearts and minds would die without. By all accounts, most demons wished me dead for my own sake. They couldn't imagine life without wings any more than I would imagine owning my place in the sky.

"You don't have to touch me." I would drag myself across the yard before I let him see how his actions had hurt me.

Clayton shifted closer, blocking the open doorway and my line of sight. His calloused fingers trailed my cheek, smoothing across my lower lip. "It's not that I don't want to touch you."

"But now you've felt them." I stiffened, trying to brace myself for his pity and unable to stop myself from adding, "I can't help it. They're a part of me."

"Shhh," he whispered, brushing his lips against my eyes where salty tears mingled with muddy rainwater. "You misunderstand me. I'm afraid if I touch you again..." his stubbled cheek rubbed against mine, "...I might not be able to stop."

My mouth fell open and he took it as an invitation, nuzzling his way across my nose until he reached my lips and sealed our mouths together with a kiss that curled my toes.

I'd never been kissed. Not with tongue and teeth and carnal intent. The rush of possibilities I'd never considered was dizzying. Heat licked along my spine and pooled lower, searing me with the need to taste more of him.

"Maddie!" my sister cried out from behind the mountain of demon thrusting his tongue inside my mouth. "Maddie! Thank Zaniah you're all right."

Clayton eased away, nipping my bottom lip as he went. The interruption saved me from making awkward excuses for my behavior or apologies for whatever had passed between us. Emma shoved him aside, scowling, and then wrapped me in a spine-snapping hug.

"I'm fine." Fine seemed like light years away from where I'd been only a few hours earlier. I stiffened, finding her embrace less comforting than it had always been.

Emma's arms fell to her sides, perhaps sensing the anger waking in me. "I should have told you. I should have warned you, but I didn't think it would happen so soon."

I frowned. Jacob had sounded as if he'd had plenty of time to make his plans. Years, if his rant could be believed. So the word *soon* didn't seem to apply. "What's happening to me?"

Emma's gaze snapped to Clayton. "This is a private conversation. Can't you go be a statue somewhere else?"

He took a few steps away, enough for the illusion of privacy at least. Emma lowered her voice.

"It's been five years since your ascendancy ceremony." Twin lines appeared between her eyebrows, drawing them down. "And you've been five years without Harper."

"Okay." I drew out the word.

"Your ascendancy coincided with your first ovulation." Her warm arms encircled me, lifting me from the truck. "But, there's more to it than that."

"What don't I know?" I asked warily.

"Askaran females are only fertile for a period of four or five days once every five years. During that time, their scent will change as their body emits a pheromone designed to attract males."

I swallowed hard. "I definitely don't remember that."

"I couldn't tell you at the time." Her explanation sounded as weak as I felt. "It's an ascendant's suitor, or if a union is prearranged, her consort, who is entrusted with all aspects of her sexual education."

"And later?" My fingers tightened in the fabric of her shirt as my nails dug into her shoulder. "You couldn't have told me this before now?"

"I tried," she snapped. "You shut me down every time I broached the topic."

"I should have been told."

"Then you shouldn't have practically stuffed your fingers in your ears every time I mentioned Harper or the damned Evanti." Her jaw set. "If I said something you didn't want to hear, you'd stop talking for days. It's my fault for not pushing you sooner, I know that, and I'm sorry. I did the best I could for you, for both of us, but I'm not perfect."

"Wait." Muddled comprehension failed me. "What about Jacob? What does this have to do with the Evanti?"

"You're a half breed claimed by one of their males. Evanti customs ensure a female a period of five years to grieve over a lost mate. Since they have so few females, it's a given she will be expected to mate again to help populate the race."

Realization dawned. "You're telling me I'm what? In *heat* and *available*?"

Emma winced. "I honestly didn't think it would get so out of hand. Harper never allowed the other males around you, so I didn't know what to expect." She barely jostled me as she climbed the front-porch steps. "I think we all underestimated the intensity of your appeal."

My gaze found its way unerringly to Clayton. "So they act on impulse rather than sincere interest?"

She bobbed her head. "Taking your pheromones into consideration? They will all be affected on some level."

Clayton's lips tightened in a hard line as we walked past. I rested my weary head on Emma's shoulder and the pastry-sweet scent of home tickled my nose.

She pressed her lips to my cheek. "I love you, *vinda koosh.*"

"I know you do." I sighed.

She settled me on the couch in our tiny living room. "Let's have a look and see what the damage is." She scanned me from head to toe, eyes snagging on the cut denim where bone pierced through flesh. Regenerated skin had already begun to swallow the protrusion. We both knew what had to be done.

She glanced at me, her face impassive. "Are you ready?"

I locked my jaw. "Do it."

A crisp snap like a celery stalk breaking filled the room. I cried out as a torrent of pain swept me up and threatened to drag me under while Emma reset the broken bone. I would heal, but damn it, I would hurt too.

Clayton charged through the doorway and came to my side in an instant, grabbing Emma by the throat and lifting her from the couch. "What the hell do you think you're doing?" He gritted out the words through his clenched teeth.

I didn't have to worry about Emma. The cold sweat breaking along my spine was all for Clayton. Something menacing stirred behind those pale blue eyes of hers.

Clayton was another matter. No matter his innate strength, or the years spent training that had honed his body to rock-hard perfection, biology still insured they were unevenly matched.

She was a halfling, and he was not. If he made her mad enough, she could level him without batting an eyelash.

I threw a couch pillow at him, bringing his attention back to me and away from a fight he couldn't win. "Clayton, let her go. She had to snap the bone before it mended completely."

He blinked his eyes as if to clear them and released Emma from his hold. He backed away slowly, slipping back behind his mask of indifference. "I apologize. That was uncalled for. I should have known you would never willingly harm her."

Emma rubbed a hand across her reddened throat. "Maddie heals quickly. I'm surprised Harper never told you. When her bones are broken, they have to be reset within a couple of hours or she has to endure a solid break."

Clayton looked past her to me. "How many times have you done this?"

She snarled. "My father wanted Maddie from the first time he saw her during the summer court of her tenth year. He knew he couldn't possess her until after her ascension, so he forced me to punish her for his pleasure." Her voice cracked. "She lived apart from the rest of the court, and she was the one thing he couldn't have. When he found out she was unbreakable..." Emma shuddered and left the rest unspoken.

Clayton's gaze held mine, but I broke the stare. Ashamed of what she and I had been. What at our basest level, we still were.

He reached out to me. "Maddie, I—"

Emma shoved him back. "Don't call her that." I heard tears in her voice. "You're not Harper no matter how much you wish you were. You don't know her."

All the churning emotion, regret, concern, confusion and

something infinitely softer, sweeter, drained from his face. "Madelyn," he corrected. "I wish you a quick recovery." He turned towards the door. "I'm going to check on Jacob before heading home." His eyes gleamed sterling. "He will be punished for what he did to you."

Emma nodded and Clayton dipped his head in turn. Clearly there was much more to this story than either had told me. But answers would have to wait until the edge of pain had dulled and I could think again.

I didn't want Clayton to go, but I couldn't ask him to stay because according to Emma, his hormones would ensure he remained, whether he wanted to or not. It would be better to let him go and clear the air between us. "Thank you, Clayton, for everything."

He didn't get a chance to respond. Our screen door flew open, slapping against the kitchen wall. Dana rushed in and made a beeline to where I lay sprawled on the couch. "Oh, Maddie," she cried. "You poor little thing. When we heard the news, I was shocked."

"Were you?" I asked, but she ignored me. This morning she had tried to tell me something. I no longer had to wonder what, but whereas I could almost forgive my sister for her actions, I did wonder what Dana's reasons for withholding information were.

"Who would have thought Jacob, *our* Jacob, would react in such a way?" She took a few more hurried steps before catching sight of Clayton. Her turnabout almost gave me whiplash. She straightened her spine, thrusting her shoulders back as she ran a hand along her hair, checking her tight bun for flyaways before turning to face him instead.

"Oh, Clayton," she cooed. "You were so brave tonight. Mason and Dillon told me all about how Jacob was drinking coffee again. He knows that stuff makes him out of his mind. That boy has got to learn to read labels."

She patted his well-defined arm. "I didn't see your truck. Why don't you let me drive you out to see Jacob? That is where you're going, right? Then I'll take you right on home."

My fingernails dug into my palms. It irked me to realize if I'd been able to walk, I would have delighted in peeling her fingers away from his arm. I'd never been a fan of Dana's, but the sudden irrational urge to wedge myself between her body and Clayton's benchmarked a new level of dislike.

He nodded. "I appreciate your offer."

She hooked her arm through his, leading him like a prize stallion through the kitchen. "Come on, hon. Don't drag your feet." Her expression shifted to something like pride. "I have three little boys waiting on their momma to get home."

The way Dana stroked him, practically crawling beneath his skin, and the way he allowed it, left little doubt as to whom the sire of her Evanti triplets must be. I remembered Emma telling me the children's father had died in the same ambush that had cost us Harper. That might not have been the case.

I recalled Jacob's words. *Did you look for his face among the children? Did you find it?*

Perhaps it wasn't Harper's likeness, but Clayton's evidenced in Dana's offspring.

Emma's voice rose over the screen door flapping shut on their exit. "Let's get you up to bed. If we get you bandaged up right, you'll be walking again by tomorrow."

"Tomorrow is Wednesday." It seemed like weeks instead of hours since I'd left the house this morning.

"No. Absolutely not." She scooped me into her arms. "You are not going hiking in the morning. One small misstep and you risk a repeat fracture. You'd be stranded on the mountain, and that is not going to happen. I won't risk another Jacob finding you isolated out there."

"Yes, Mom," I quipped.

She wrinkled her nose and glanced down at my bloodied and muddied state. "Do you want to take a shower before you lie down?"

I stared longingly at my bed. With the covers pulled down and my pillow fluffed within an inch of its life, I couldn't resist its siren song. "Not tonight. I'll catch one in the morning. It's not like I have to worry about infection, and I'll wash the sheets myself so you don't have to. Besides, we've slept through worse."

And we had.

Chapter Nine

The next day my steps were slower, the burn of impact as my legs absorbed my weight more pronounced, but I was up and walking. The discomfort didn't stop me from working, but Emma tried to.

Every fifteen minutes she brought out a quart-sized freezer bag full of ice cubes and pushed me down into a booth before slapping it onto the sore knee. Lucky for us, Wednesdays were, without fail, the slowest day of the workweek.

Glass comprised two-thirds of the diner's outer wall, giving our patrons a window to the outside world. And who didn't like to people watch? I stared through the Windex-polished panes and craned my neck, trying to catch a glimpse of Emasen, but left a smear from my forehead instead.

"Stop sulking." Emma tossed a balled-up napkin at me, bouncing it off the side of my head.

I picked it up and wiped away the smudge. "I'm not sulking." Okay, so if I didn't tuck in my bottom lip, I would probably trip over it before the shift's end. "I haven't missed a cliff day since coming here."

The mountain had been my place of solace in a time when I'd needed a way to cope. On the rare occasions when Mother allowed me to travel in Rihos, Harper had sneaked me to a barren summit neighboring the summer castle.

I would sit, dangling my feet over the ledge and watch as he dived into open air and raced towards the ground in freefall. I gasped each time as his wings snapped open with a sharp *pop* to halt his descent.

Sometimes, he had even cradled me against him, allowing me to play the game too.

I needed a way to forget I'd cost such a vibrant male his life. Emasen gave that to me. There, I could almost hear his laughter carried on the winds roaring through the basin.

I exhaled slowly, taking stock of how I'd squandered the life he'd given me. I'd done nothing, went nowhere to justify his sacrifice. My chest ached. My heart hurt until I wished to pull it out and slide back down into the mire of my self-imposed isolation.

My fingernails bit into my palms. No, I would use the pain to anchor me. To keep me awakened and remind me of the high cost of freedom and the male who'd paid the price so I didn't have to.

"More icing and less pouting." Emma pointed to where the bag only half covered my knee.

I straightened the compress and cast a quick glance around the diner. An elderly couple hunching over their bowls of soup du jour were the lunch rush today. The rest of the place sat empty, and had been since the sparse morning rush.

"Can I ask you something?" I tore the napkin into little strips and tried to shore up my courage. I wanted to ask about Clayton. What he was like, where he went, what he did. Anything to get insight on the male who'd consumed my dreams last night.

Even as I told myself I wanted his friendship to cement a fragile tie to Harper, I knew it was a lie. I wanted him for purely selfish reasons having nothing to do with his brother and everything to do with how I'd felt in his arms last night.

Emma wiped her hands with a rag threaded through her apron loop. "Shoot."

"Do you think that I'll see Clayton again? Is he...?"

The way her nostrils flared made me rethink my question. Emma definitely had some kind of history with him, and it didn't appear to be the happy kind. I wanted to ask if he and Dana were attached, but chickened out and jerked a thumb towards table five.

"It's been fifteen minutes. I bet Mr. Jenkins is tapping his foot and checking his watch. You better top off his coffee soon if you want to earn that ten-cent tip."

Emma glanced over, chuckling. "You're so bad." But she picked up the last pot of coffee off the line and carried it over to the waiting gentleman, using the final drops to refill his cup.

I exhaled once she walked out of hearing range.

The muffled ring of the telephone cut through the silence. "You want me to get that?"

She topped off the almost level mug of coffee and walked back to the bar to set the pot on the counter. "Nice try, but you have ten minutes left. Don't move a muscle or I'll make you sit out another ten just for spite."

I shrugged and let my head rest against the vinyl seatback. A minute or two passed while I considered whether or not rephrasing my question might help deflect some of her anger. When she rounded the corner, worry knitted her forehead. Her hands fumbled with her apron strings, caught between untying them and making the knots worse.

"Are you okay? Who was on the phone?"

"That was Dana." She dropped her hands. "Apparently Parker took a dare from one or both of his brothers to fly up to the roof of the inn."

I sat upright. "Is he okay? Did they get him down?"

"He's down all right. He got scared and fell off the edge. Dana sounded certain his leg is broken. She wanted to know if I could baby-sit the inn and the guilty parties while she drives Parker to the emergency room."

I shooed her with my hands, poised to pull off the icepack. "Go on." I gestured towards the vacant restaurant. "It's not like there's anything happening here. Besides, you'll be right across the street."

"I can't leave you alone. Anything could happen. Maybe Lynn could come in for the last half of the shift. It's only a few hours. Her male can live without her that long."

The tinkle of the tiny silvery bell hung over the entrance intruded into our conversation. We both glanced over, expecting to see one of the regulars, but finding Clayton instead.

He nodded to Emma before shooting me a dimpled grin. My heart skipped faster and my hands turned clammy. The taste of his impulsive kiss from the night before seemed to flavor my tongue. I didn't know what to say to him.

Emma didn't have that problem. "What do you think you're doing here?"

He held up a bouquet of daisies. The multicolored kind you bought at the grocery store and wondered if nature or food coloring lent them their vibrancy. A tiny rectangle of cardstock peeked just over the top with the words "Get Well Soon" emblazoned on them.

"I came to see how Madelyn was feeling today."

He crossed the restaurant, bypassed a none-too-pleased Emma, and sat on the bench opposite me. He offered me the flowers with a quick jut of his arm. Maybe he was embarrassed, which I'm sure had nothing to do with my sister standing just over his shoulder, staring daggers at his back.

When I took the bouquet, our fingers met around the bundled stems and the spark of something arced between us.

"Thank you." The scent of permanent marker used to sign his name to the card made my nose wrinkle.

"You're welcome. How are you feeling?"

"Sore, but I've felt worse." I tried to soften that truth with a smile, but I don't think either of them bought it. I ushered Emma with my hands. "Parker's waiting. You'd better go."

Clayton asked, "What happened to Parker?"

I worded my answer carefully. "He fell from the inn's roof and probably broke his leg when he landed. Emma"—I gave her my most severe look—"is going to cover for Dana while she takes him in to the hospital."

I watched for his reaction. He frowned over the news, but didn't dash from the diner or ask to make a phone call. I couldn't see a male like Clayton not caring for his offspring, so his casual acceptance of Parker's injury made me question my hasty judgment. Maybe he wasn't their father after all.

Emma's hard stare dragged me from my thoughts. "I haven't decided if I'm going or not. I don't want to leave you alone." She dug in her pockets. "I'll see if Lynn or Marci are home."

Clayton's gaze touched on points around the open eat-in area. "I haven't been here in years." His lips tipped up in a smile reminiscent of a child caught doing something bad. "I do have Dana sneak me hamburgers from time to time. The food here is the best in town." He cleared his throat. "If you don't mind having a trainee underfoot, I'd be glad to stay and help out. That way Emma could leave and you wouldn't be alone."

"That would be—"

"No, absolutely not," she snapped, holding the phone to her ear. "Damn it, is no one ever at home when you need them?"

I groaned. "You need to go. There's a five-year-old boy in pain, waiting on you to get your butt in gear. Clayton is already here and the inn is *just across the street.*"

As she looked through the window, I saw her resolve weaken and the phone flip closed. "Fine, but you keep your phone on and in your pocket. Call me if he so much as looks at you funny."

"Will do." I offered her a mock salute.

She spared another second to glare at Clayton before pushing through the front door, jogging across the pavement and disappearing inside the modest house turned local inn.

He drummed his fingers on the tabletop. "So, what does a waiter-in-training do around here?"

I pointed towards the bar. "He puts on a pot of fresh coffee. Emma just poured the last drop." I paused. "Are you okay to be around it?"

"I had my round with caffeine a long time ago." He laughed softly. "My father beat that addiction right out of my hide."

His joking tone led me to believe his beatings were of a different sort than the ones I'd grown up experiencing. But the subject of his father did make me wonder. "Was he a hard man?"

Clayton shrugged. "He was a lot of things, but yes, hard was one of them." He pushed away from the table and any other questions I might have asked. His skilled avoidance of subjects he didn't want to talk about with me only succeeded in making me more curious about him. "Is there anything else that needs doing?"

I swallowed noticeably. "Just listen out for the bell over the door. Nurse Emma says I'm booth bound for at least another five minutes."

"Good for her. You need to rest that knee."

Despite the dull throb in my knee, I felt fine. I could have gone hiking today. I would go hiking tomorrow, whether my sister approved of it or not. My skin itched from being confined to small spaces. I wanted fresh air and sunshine, not recycled blasts from the circulating heat vents and fluorescent lighting.

"I'm perfectly fine." I balled up the mess I'd made in my palm. "There's no reason I couldn't be at Emasen instead of here."

"Emasen?"

"Yes, I hike Emasen, thank you very much. Every Wednesday, except today because of yesterday's...mishap."

"That's a very dangerous pass. You're better off waiting until you can handle it."

"You know what?" I snatched the bag of ice from my knee and slid from the booth. "Never mind about the coffee, I'll get it myself."

My uneven stride was worsened by my frozen-stiff kneecap. Instead of storming off into the kitchen, it was more of an undignified hobbling. I snatched the empty pot off the counter and went into the kitchen to give it a quick rinse in the stainless-steel sink. The dull roar of high water pressure meeting sink basin meant I didn't hear Clayton follow me.

I did feel him tug the end of my long braid to get my attention. I twisted around to face him and found he still held the rope of hair in his hand.

"Is there something I can help you with?" I planted my feet, determined not to find the way his broad shoulders hemmed me in unnerving.

He shrugged, still fingering the ends. "I have a confession to make." His voice wavered with the same indecision causing me to slip on my first attempt to turn off the faucet. I picked at my fingernails to avoid looking into his face.

"Okay, let's hear it."

I could have kicked myself for prompting him, but he made me curious. I couldn't imagine anything making this male nervous, but I saw the fine tremors move through his hand. He disguised it by fumbling my braid.

"I used to watch you."

I tore my nail down to the quick and cursed as a perfect blood drop formed on my finger. "Damn it." It stung, but was hardly life threatening. Determined, I still played up the wound to make the most of his momentary shift in focus. I needed a minute. Sixty minutes wouldn't be enough to pull order from the chaos of my thoughts.

Clayton lifted my hand to his opened mouth. His lips closed around my finger. My eyes fluttered shut before I could stop them. When his tongue swirled around my finger, my other hand grasped the sink for support. I didn't want him to stop.

I bit back a moan. "You watched me?"

He released my finger with a kiss to the tip. His shoulders rolled. "I tried not to. I knew I shouldn't, but I couldn't help myself."

His downcast eyes and guilty expression softened me. I tipped his chin up with my finger. "Why are you doing this? We hardly know one another."

He turned his cheek into my hand so that I flattened my palm against his rugged jaw. The same heat from the night before rekindled, roaring to life. "I know you don't know me," he said. "But the way Harper talked about you...I feel as if I know you, like I've always known you."

His strong thumbs rolled over the joints in my fingers. "I know that you grew lilacs in a planter box outside of your bedroom window in Rihos." I barely noticed his subtle shift closer. "And that Harper knocked it loose learning to fly so that it always tilted to one side."

The center of my chest filled with something achingly sweet. He knew me in the same way I knew him, through snippets of conversation and shared spaces. How many times had we walked down a common path without our lives crossing? How many times had he made certain they didn't?

I noticed we now stood chest to chest. "I don't know—"

"Just give me a chance." He coaxed my hand from his face to drape it across his shoulder. "I promise you won't regret it."

I had time. If I hadn't wanted what he offered, I could have stopped him then and there, but I didn't. I couldn't. Under his fingers, my senses awakened with a deep stirring I wanted to experience. I needed to feel that way again.

His dark head lowered, lips parting just before they reached mine. The first light tease of his mouth across mine had my fingers digging into his shirt. His touch was gentle, asking. I answered the only way I could. Grasping his shoulder, I urged him down to me.

When his tongue thrust through my parted lips, I moaned and leaned into him. He backed me until his hips pinned mine to the sink basin. Pleasure preceded panic as his large body corralled mine. Maybe I wasn't ready. This could be a huge mistake. He might not even realize what he was asking.

"We can't just," I gasped. "There are customers out there and they might need me."

"I need you more than they do." His lips rejoined mine,

kissing me once, twice.

I wanted to believe him, but how could I? I couldn't forgive myself if I took advantage of him while my body coursed with pheromones designed to make him act this way. I broke away from him, needing space to clear my head.

The shop's bell tinkled, followed by the low hum of eager, excited voices.

Relieved by the interruption, I seized the opportunity with both hands. "What is all that noise? One of us needs to go find out." I walked towards the hall, but his muscular arm braced across the doorway and blocked me inside the kitchen.

"It sounds almost like..." He stuck his head out to look around the corner. "It is." He sighed and adjusted a bulge in his pants that hadn't been there moments before. My gaze darted away quickly. Not that I had been looking. "Oh, hell, it's a busload of kids. I see a couple dozen and they're still coming."

Clayton thumped his forehead against the wooden trim of the doorway. His expression turned so dire, I grinned. I couldn't help it.

"Come on, waiter boy. Let's see what you're made of. Surely, the colony leader can handle a couple dozen kids looking for the chicken snack special?"

I fished a pad and pen from my pocket and offered them to him. He took them with a resigned grunt as I grabbed his arms and twisted him around to face the hall. "It's easy. You seat them in groups of four until we run out of booths, then you move on to tables. Then you ask, 'What would you like to drink?' Hand out the menus—wait five minutes and ask, 'Are you ready to order?'"

He spun around and reeled me against him, capturing my mouth with his. I raised my fingers to touch where my lips still tingled. "What was that for?"

"Luck."

Supplies in hand, he went to face our customers while I turned up the fryer and added more oil. Then I hauled out bags of frozen French fries and baggies full of Emma's special-recipe chicken strips from the walk-in freezer.

I paused as I heard Clayton's raised voice drift down the short hall. "What would you like to drink?" he asked, followed by a cacophony of noise as dozens of children answered all in the same breath.

I chuckled, almost feeling sorry for him as I dropped the first batch of chicken into the grease.

Hours later, the kids were gone, the tables cleared, the floors mopped and the closed sign flipped over.

Clayton sank into a worn dining chair just inside the kitchen. "I don't see how you do that every day."

I looked up from loading the dishwasher. "It's not that intense every day. Mainly on weekends or the odd holiday, but most days it's not a bad way to make a living. I enjoy it."

The heavier pans clattered as I dropped them into the deep, industrial-grade sink.

"Can I give you a hand with those?"

"Sure." I paused, considering. "You do know how to wash dishes, right?"

A few feet above the sink hung a coil of ribbed silver tubing ending in a spray nozzle. The premise was simple. You pulled and water came out of the end.

"I have washed dishes before, you know. You have to learn a lot of things living on your own, but I guess I don't have to tell you that."

"Fine," I said, unconvinced. "Show me."

He reached up and gave a swift yank on the bell-shaped

head, activating the sprayer at full power. I heard the water bounce off the metal pans still crusted with biscuits left over from breakfast. His hand opened and the cord pulled taut, retracting as he cursed and jumped backwards.

When he turned around, his white polo shirt was slicked to his stomach, and I could count the ridges of muscles in his abdomen. He was soaked from chest to crotch. I cleared my throat and found something interesting in the doodling around our shift schedule to hold my attention.

"It's stronger than what I'm used to, okay?"

Between his defensive tone, his confounded expression and his soaked clothes, I couldn't help it. I laughed. It was easy to relax with him. He uncorked all the laughter I'd bottled up over the last few years until it released in a rush that cramped my stomach as I doubled over, gasping for breath.

His hand lifted, going for the sprayer again. Instinct told me to run and run fast before he had the chance to do whatever it was making his eyes gleam and his lips hitch up to one side.

I spun around and barely made the doorway just before a stream of icy water hit the small of my back. Water seeped into my pants and soaked my underwear, running down my legs until even my shoes squelched.

"What was that for?" Now the loose shirt I wore over my tank top clung to my skin.

"Payback." His lips formed a wicked grin.

"I didn't do anything to get paid back for. You were the one who said he knew how to work the sprayer." I fumbled the hair band from my braid and finger combed the length until it covered my soaked back.

"You laughed at me."

"It was funny."

He grabbed the hose again. "I'll be more careful this time."

"No." I backed out of range just in case he got any ideas. "Just leave them. I'll do it. Just let me mop up this mess first." I took a step and slipped a fraction, wincing when my bad knee sailed out from under me.

Clayton cleared the distance in four swift strides. He bent down, getting level with my stomach, and hauled me up over his shoulder. "I made the mess. I'll clean it up. Just tell me where the mop is."

I pounded my balled-up fists against his back. "Put me down. Now. Or I'm calling Emma."

"Tattletale," he teased, and swatted my bottom with his open hand.

"Oww." I would have fought harder if I hadn't looked down and noticed the bunch and flex of his ass moving beneath the faded denim of his jeans. I was tempted to reach down and give his bottom a good, solid whack, but I didn't want to encourage him.

He carried me to the front of the diner and dropped me into a booth. "You stay put."

I couldn't believe his audacity. I jumped to my feet and got in his face. "You are not the boss of me." I jabbed his solid chest with my finger. "I don't need two mother hens. Emma's constant clucking is bad enough."

It was a mistake to stand so close to him, but I couldn't remember why when his palms cupped my cheeks and his lips dipped down to cover mine.

I broke the kiss. "You can't keep kissing me to shut me up."

He turned my face back to his. "Then shut up so I can kiss you."

The slow brush of his lips over mine made me realized how

dead I'd been inside. Sure, I'd eaten and slept, talked and walked, worked—but I hadn't cared if I stopped doing any of those things. Now I needed them. The awakening that had begun last night in the burrow culminated now in his presence.

I burned, hot and insistent, craving things I'd never imagined. Like the coarse scrub of his hands over my skin or the soft sounds he made when I kissed him back. Little things that told me how he felt without him saying a word.

He lifted me onto the tabletop, bringing me closer to his searching mouth. His fingers slid up my ribs, almost touching, but not quite where I wanted them to be. The front of my shirt was damp from being carried against his soaked clothing. The wet fabric and cool air puckered my nipples, making them tighten, drawing them to the heat of his widespread hands.

"Am I supposed to feel like I'm on fire?" I asked as his teeth closed over the skin of my neck. "I've never felt like this before."

He growled. "God, that's what I want to hear."

I pushed him back, glancing over my shoulder. "There's nothing but glass behind us." Just because I couldn't see anyone beyond the diner's lights didn't mean they weren't there.

"Please, Maddie." His sincere tone was my undoing. "Let me have a little more."

I pushed down my instinctive rejection, the uncertainties, everything blocking my enjoyment of the moment. I felt certain I would think clearer after he had left and taken his sweet temptations with him.

"Okay."

His dark laughter at my acceptance should have worried me, would have if I'd been able to think past the pleasure of holding his firm male body against mine. Of feeling his heart race and his breath catch when I nipped his bottom lip in repayment for the night before.

I had the fleeting thought that Harper had never stirred this side of me. Then Clayton's head lowered and his teeth claimed my taut nipple through the fabric of my damp shirt and my mind flipped off like a thrown switch.

His hands smoothed below the wet tail of my shirt and spanned my rib cage before heading higher and pushing my bra upward until my breasts were freed.

"Can I taste you?" he asked.

I nodded since my tongue seemed paralyzed. Maybe I'd bitten it. Maybe he had. I didn't know and I didn't care.

He tugged my shirt up just high enough he could reach bare skin. When his lips closed over my breast, his teeth tugging the taut peak, I gasped and arched closer.

His low hum of approval made my fever burn higher. My eager hands reached for him, fingers seeking purchase in his soggy shirt, but he was already pulling away.

"No." He caught them and lifted them both to his lips, pressing a kiss into each palm. "Not this time." He gently lowered the cups of my bra back into place and smoothed my shirt down before sinking to his knees and wrapping his palms around my calves. His cheek settled across the top of my thigh.

His breaths were shallow, rapid, his hold tight and fingers pinching.

"Are you okay?" I asked breathlessly, uncertain of what had just happened. Or not happened.

"I just—I didn't mean to take things so far."

I tensed as doubt wormed its way back into my mind. Could pheromones be to blame for this driving need between us? My gut clinched at the thought.

He stroked the inside of my thigh with his thumb. "I know what you're thinking. It's not the pheromones. I stopped

because you're important to me and I don't want to push you."
He glanced up and I watched hope and fear and a dozen smaller
emotions flicker across his face. "If we pursue this, I need to
know it's me you want."

His gaze broke from mine when he dropped his cheek back
to rest on my leg. I twisted a few of his dark curls around my
finger and scratched my blunt nails across his scalp. "I
understand."

Better than he realized. He might fear I saw him as a
replacement for Harper, but I feared he didn't see me at all. I
wanted us both to be certain, conscious of the choices we made.

The light creak of hinges and the high scrape of metal drew
my attention towards the hall. I glanced away from Clayton in
time to see Emma weaving her way around upturned chairs
placed on tabletops. Since I had her keys, she must have made
the long trip around to the emergency exit.

"What exactly do you think you're doing, Clayton?"

He still hadn't looked up.

"He's not doing anything wrong." I petted his hair. "We were
just talking."

She snorted. "*Talking* doesn't leave my kitchen six inches
underwater. *Talking* doesn't leave two full-grown demons
soaking wet. Unless you were both pretending to be mermaids
trying to perfect freshwater communication in my sink, I fail to
see how *talking* had anything to do with whatever you two were
up to."

Clayton's head lifted just before he stood. "I'll clean up the
mess."

"No, you'll go home and let me take care of Maddie. She
could have slipped and hurt herself again."

I wasn't about to tell her that's how we had ended up in

here. His face blanked, telling me he was thinking the same thing, probably blaming himself too.

"Fine." He sounded tired all of a sudden. "I'll leave."

He bent down to press a quick kiss to my cheek. "I enjoyed today. It was fun, except for the screaming kids and spilled drinks." While at my ear, he whispered, "Can I see you again?"

I nodded, brushing our cheeks together.

"Soon?" he asked.

"Soon." I pulled him in for a hug. "Thanks for sticking around. I had fun too."

Emma cleared her throat. "If you two don't mind, I'd like to get home sometime before midnight."

When he pulled back, I let him go and watched as he walked out the back door Emma had left ajar.

"Stop staring and roll your tongue back into your mouth."

"I'm not staring." I slid down from my perch. "I'll help you clean up."

"No, you stay put. It's a slick and soapy mess back there. It will only take longer if I have to watch your every step."

I dropped down into the booth. For once, I wouldn't argue.

My time with Clayton had given me plenty to ponder...and desire.

Chapter Ten

The next morning, warmth from a body curled intimately into my side radiated a delicious sense of peace, enveloping me deeper into sleep. Rolling over, I snuggled closer to the source and buried my face in sweetly scented fur. A few chaste licks swiped across my parted lips, snapping me into consciousness. Blinking against the bright morning sun, I locked onto a pair of dark, chocolate eyes staring languidly back at me across my pillow.

"Good morning." The dog's thin lips curled into an unnatural smile, white fangs gleaming.

The scream that ripped from my throat came loud and long as I rolled over, falling off the bed and landing in a sprawl across the hardwood floor. A tiny wagging bundle of fluff bounced joyfully across the bed to stand, staring down at me, from the mattress's edge. It cocked its head enquiringly to one side as soft puppy breath blew warm air into my face.

I clamped a hand over my mouth to muffle the screams that sounded pathetic even to my ears. I'd known Emma wanted me to have some kind of companion, but what was that thing? Dogs didn't look like that. It was too hairy, like a mop come to life, and its eyes were too bright. It looked entirely too happy to see me.

The bedroom door burst open as Emma fell through to land

on the floor beside me in a tangle of pajamas. We both stared at the doorknob lodged firmly in the drywall. She squinted against the sun, lifting a hand to ward off the overly bright rays.

"What happened?" Her words mashed together. "Are you all right?" She grunted and got back on her feet. "What's going on in here?"

I raised a shaky hand to point at the shaggy occupant of the bed. "*That* caught me off guard."

Emma's expression shifted from dazed to pure delight as she knelt to pat the monster responsible for rousing me from sleep. "Aww, you have a puppy. Where did she come from?"

"I—I thought you bought her for me, as a gift or something."

She cut her eyes to me. "I'm not that mean. I know you didn't want a pet." She continued to ruffle the dog's glossy fur. "Even though this one is a cutie."

The tiny beast bounced up and down in adulation as she washed Emma's cheek with her long pink tongue. Tossing a glance over her doggy shoulder, the animal shot me a conspiratorial wink.

A cold dread flooded me. I felt ill. It couldn't be. Could it? "That dog just winked at me."

"Don't be silly," she chided. "Dogs can't wink." She scratched behind the animal's ears as it emitted a throaty rumble. "Don't take this the wrong way, but I think your dog just purred at me." She laughed.

Now my sister was making fun of me. "That is *not* my dog," I complained as I got to my feet and stood at the foot of the bed.

She ignored me, speaking to the pooch instead. "How did you get in here?" The puppy snuffled her hand. "If she's not yours, then whose is she?" She tickled it behind the ears, more concerned about the dog than me. That shift in attention grated since I knew the *puppy* was milking it for all it was worth.

Glaring at the smiling doggy face, I shrugged noncommittally. I could tell Emma to ask the dog herself, but then she would think my night in the woods had been more traumatic than I'd admitted. No normal person spoke to animals. Period. And worse, to reveal that they answered me was a certificate to the loony bin. *Not wise, Maddie. Not wise at all.* Best keep that tidbit secret for now...or forever.

"What's this?" Emma drew my attention back to her new best friend. "I didn't notice you had a collar." Her fingers slid around a bright red band hidden in the thick fur. "I guess coffee really is what jumpstarts my brain in the morning."

I.D. tags glinted on her palm as she turned them over to look for a name. I knew that the tags had not been there moments before. My world was spinning wildly out of control. I dropped my forehead into my hands, smothering the insane need to giggle. Thankfully, Emma wasn't firing on all cylinders. When I peeked through my fingers, she had pinched the tag, worrying the smooth surface with her thumb.

"I bet your owner is worried sick about you," she cooed in a baby-talk voice I'd heard her use on Dana's children. "Hmm."

"What is it?" I inched nearer, hoping it wasn't a step closer to madness.

"If found please contact Clayton Delaney," she read. An angry jerk of her hand let the tags drop back into place. She stared at the dog as if it had grown a second head.

Knowledge hammered at my brain, filling my aching head to the bursting point. The dog's russet coat gleamed with health and her eyes shined with preternatural intelligence. "Figment?"

Her head tilted to one side curiously as her tail thumped the bed. She acknowledged my recognition although unfamiliar with the name I called her.

Emma looked at me thoughtfully, almost suspiciously. "Is that her name?" Her eyebrow arched. "I thought you didn't know this dog—or who owns her."

"I don't." I cleared my throat to hide my anxiety. "Do you know Clayton's number off the top of your head?"

"No, and only his name is listed on the tags. No address or phone number."

A sharp snap of fingers vibrated inside my head.

"I knew I'd forgotten something."

Emma didn't flinch or jump back and pull the "you talked" routine like I had two days before. She hadn't heard a darn thing. Her hands stayed buried in thick, silky pelt as she scratched the wriggling dog. Great, this proved insanity really was a one-way ticket and I was the only passenger riding the train.

Figment bounded towards me, twisting the sheets and pawing at my plush comforter. She turned her head back towards Emma, where I was certain she practiced her cheesiest doggy grin. Emma lit up, smiling and suddenly willing to forgive the puppy her ownership. With her front paws, Figment rummaged in the comforter, pulling it aside to nuzzle a bright red cellular phone.

"Whose is that?" Emma knew full well it wasn't my phone. She had purchased my new purple RAZR only a few months earlier.

"I have no idea." I didn't want to know where the phone came from; I just wanted it to go back. A snippet of rock music blared in timed bursts as it vibrated under Figment's possessive paw.

Emma glanced at the phone. "Well, aren't you going to

answer it?"

I reached to tug it away from Figment, who sat back to watch, looking much too smug for my comfort. Pressing the send button, I managed a stunted greeting. "Hello?"

A male's gravelly voice stabbed back. "Hello?"

"Who is this?" I felt a sick, sinking twist in my chest descending into my stomach. The sensation was like dozens of butterfly wings were tickling my insides before deciding it would be more fun to ram the lining of my stomach to punch their way out to freedom. Maybe I was just hungry. Only my stomach wasn't growling. Just wringing itself tighter and tighter as silence on the line lingered.

"This is Clayton." Sleep honeyed his voice thick and deep, enticing. "Who am I talking to?"

"This is Madelyn." I stupidly tacked on, "Toliver." And just to make sure he could add two and two together, I elaborated further. "Madelyn Toliver, Emma's sister, you stayed with me at the diner yesterday?" *What a lame thing to say.*

"I remember." His husky chuckle reminded me of exactly what we'd done last night. "And I'm glad you called, even if it is early."

Instant denial sprang from my lips. "I didn't call."

"But my phone rang..." He allowed the sentence to hang unfinished.

I glared at Figment. Certain blame for both the phone and the call could be laid at her paws.

Emma poked my arm and mouthed the word "Clayton." I nodded. Her lips twisted into an impressive snarl. She lunged for the phone, bracing her hand on my shin. I'm not proud of how I faked a wince or how Emma shrank back looking worried she had caused me even one more ounce of pain. "Look, I'm sorry for the confusion, but I found your dog."

"You found my dog?" His deadpan delivery called my mental state into question not for the first time in the past three days.

He almost had me believing the problem was mine alone. "Yes, your *dog*."

"Oh."

Oh? I leaned down, taking the dog's tag between my fingers as tangible proof of my sanity. "I have a dog sitting on my bed wearing a collar that says, 'If found please call Clayton Delaney.'"

He didn't speak for several heartbeats. I matched the time as I counted mine thudding loudly in my ears. "I'll be right over. Just let me pull on some clothes first," he finally replied.

The vision my mind conjured up of Clayton naked made me forget to breathe. All that dark skin peeking out from a tangle of sheets caught around his waist. I thought about his appearance from the night before and wondered if he slept with glamour or without.

My cheeks flamed, drawing Emma's attention like a magnet. "Okay. Bye," I managed to squeak out as I pressed the end button in panic. He had to have heard the tremor in my voice before the connection died.

"Well?" Her eyes narrowed in suspicion. "What did he say?"

"He's on his way over to pick up his..." I leveled a stony glare at the current bane of my sanity, "...dog."

I had to distract her before the questions became too probing. Emma's knowing eyes were on me as I took in the disheveled state of my hair with a few pats to my sleep-tangled head and glanced down at my worn pajamas. "I need to take a shower and get into some fresh clothes before our guest arrives."

Emma patted her new fawning friend before moving to the doorway. "All right, I'll start breakfast while you get cleaned up. See you in a few."

She left me with Figment. "You're not real."

Her brown eyes rolled. *"I'm just as real as you are."*

That was hardly a ringing endorsement. "So you belong to Clayton?"

She nodded. *"You don't have to vocalize, you know."*

"I prefer to," came my gruff answer. "Does he know?" I waved my hand in a circular whoop-de-do motion. "Of course he knows you can talk. He didn't try to have me committed for telling him to come get his..." I inserted air quotes, "...'dog', because the psych ward would have had to bring a straitjacket built for two."

"Please don't be mad at me."

"I'm not mad at you." I sighed, running a hand over my eyes and the crumbling flakes of sleep dried there. "I have to take a shower."

"Okay." Figment's tongue lolled in agreement as she jumped down from the bed and trotted to the bathroom on my heels.

I came to an abrupt halt. Her wet nose jabbed into my calf. "I'm going to shower. Alone, if you don't mind." I gestured towards the bed. "You wait out here. You are not coming in with me."

"Why not?"

"I will be naked." Not that dozens of people hadn't seen me naked, and hundreds more seen me nearly naked for ritual's sake. I just preferred not to add needlessly to that number.

Her amber eyes glittered. *"I've seen Clayton naked."*

Thanks for that, I thought to myself.

"You're welcome."

"Get out of my head, will you." My growl was getting worse than my bite.

"Okay. But about him being naked..."

Saliva pooled in my mouth, forcing me to swallow or risk my second drowning in forty-eight hours. This was not what I needed at the moment. "Lucky you. Now scoot. I want privacy, unlike your precious Clayton."

Her tone turned confiding. *"He doesn't look the same way a female does, you know."*

I didn't want to know why she knew what Clayton looked like nude or why she sounded so puzzled over the differences in male and female anatomy. Even worse, I didn't want to know the naked female in question. "I should hope so." Unbidden, thoughts of Clayton twined with Dana flashed through my mind, ruining the fantasy I had created.

I shoved Figment across the threshold into the bedroom with a thrust of my foot, closing the bathroom door firmly behind her. A quick twist of vintage, four-pronged handles made water rush from the bathtub's faucet. I tweaked until I had the temperature perfect. The steam even seemed to help relax me from the shock of seeing Figment again. I stepped into the clawfoot tub and pulled the metal pin, activating the shower. I could almost hear my skin sizzle under the cascade of hot water.

Scrubbing my hair and humming along, I shivered when a cool blast of air sucked the warmth from the room. I looked towards the door even though it was obscured by the opaque shower curtain and got an eyeful of shampoo for my trouble.

"Did you finish cooking already?" Eyes stinging, I jerked open the shower curtain and groped blindly for the towel bar.

133

"Can you hand me that towel? This Tea Tree stuff burns."

A harsh intake of breath drew my burning eyes open in alarm. Instead of my sister, Clayton's wide-set shoulders filled the entrance to my tiny bathroom. His death grip on the doorknob loosened as he reached to toss a bundle of warm terrycloth into my waiting arms.

"Damn it." His gaze cut to the floor. His finger pointed down at Figment. "She told me you expected me. I didn't mean to—"

"You didn't mean to play peeping Tom?" I used the towel he'd tossed to wipe my face. Seeking refuge behind the curtain, I tossed the towel over the curtain rod at the far end of the tub.

Clayton growled. "The door was already open. I stepped over to shut it when you opened the shower curtain."

I stepped beneath the gentle spray to rinse my hair and give myself a moment to think. "How convenient for you," I said loud enough to be heard over the cascading water. I was going to strangle Figment. If Clayton had found the door open, somehow I knew she was to blame. "And you couldn't have said something?"

He didn't respond. At first, I thought he must have left. I bent down and turned off the water. Peering around the curtain's edge, I found Clayton standing right where I'd left him.

Molten black pools crashed into mine. His true self stared out where blue eyes should be. His lips parted slightly. I could almost hear his erratic heart rate bouncing across the small space between us.

"I'm sorry. I didn't mean to barge in uninvited."

I waved away his apology as the last shred of my feminine mystique flew out the window. "No problem. I'm sure a savvy, earth-dwelling male such as you has seen plenty of prime female assets before. Mine don't rate a second glance." I blotted my face again before clutching the plush towel across my chest.

"I'm sure I don't have anything you haven't seen before." Only I did, so I arranged the towel to drape across my shoulders and cover the curve of my spine.

Before either of us compounded the awkwardness of the situation, Emma barreled into the room, catching a glimpse of me, mostly naked, over Clayton's shoulder.

"What the hell are you doing up here?" Lavender runes crept across her face, swirling angrily as her glamour shorted out in her rage.

The same question had plagued me as well. More to the point, I wondered how he would blame Figment, the seemingly innocent dog, for being caught trespassing.

Clayton's voice was curt. "I saw my dog run up the stairs and I followed. Finding Madelyn this way was incidental."

Emma's pointer fingernail lengthened to a razor-sharp claw. She tapped once against his chest, slicing through the tailored dress shirt like a hot knife through butter. "Incidental? How very convenient. Haven't you heard of knocking before entering?" she snarled. "You don't just come barging into other people's homes. You wait for an invitation." She tapped again, this time drawing a fine line of blood.

I cleared my throat, hoping to lighten the tension crackling thick and fast between them. "Um, hello? I'm trying to dry off here." Neither responded, and both ignored the squeak of my bare feet leaving tub for tile.

I cast around for a secondary towel or scrap of clothing. There was nothing besides the empty hamper and the scent of pine cleaner from Emma's daily cleansing regimen. Abandoning hope of making a concealed getaway, I pulled the towel tighter across my shoulders, turned sideways and slipped through the narrow gap left between Clayton's body and the doorway.

An almost imperceptible shiver coursed through him. My

nipples puckered into tight buds. The slide of skin on skin seared me where I'd brushed past his arm and felt the rake of his coarse hairs over my soft flesh.

His stare branded me like a tangible caress, marking me as his. My legs wobbled unsteadily as I stepped away. Turning, I faced him before dropping my towel, carefully keeping my back to the wall. I slowly pulled panties up my thighs and hooked my bra in front before twisting it around back. Instinct made me seek revenge on his intrusion by teasing his senses with each slow tug of satin over my curves.

Emma snarled threateningly. "Don't look at her like that."

He did not avert his face. "Like what?" he asked, his eyes never leaving me.

"Like you just ate dinner and she's the dessert." Emma shoved him backwards. "She is untouched—"

This was becoming humiliating. I tuned out their argument as I zipped up jeans and shrugged into a cap-sleeve shirt. Clayton knew Harper and I never physically crossed the finish line. Just like he had to know, because of my stigma, no one else would have wanted me beyond furthering their social aspirations. But still—I'd rather not be present while my virtue was brought up for debate.

The aroma of bacon wafted up from downstairs. My tummy rumbled in response. "I'm heading down for breakfast." I waited for a response. They ignored me.

Emma crawled into Clayton's face, twisting her sharpened finger into his chest. "You can't be a part of her life." I half expected to see her hand emerge through his back. She was pushing that hard.

He leaned down, bringing them nose to nose. "I won't hide myself from her any longer."

I didn't see what difference it could possibly make. I knew

about him now. That cat was out of the bag. "Breakfast anyone?" I grabbed my hairbrush and combed out the long, wet locks. "Any takers?"

I shrugged and left them to it, taking the stairs down to the first floor and walking into the kitchen. Here, the scent of fried bacon, sausage, eggs seasoned with peppers and onions mingled with the fragrance of buttery biscuits cooling on a rack. Even a tiny boiler filled with sugared grits sat cooling off to one side of the stove.

I spooned some of the scrambled mixture onto a plate, then grabbed a clean spoon and added grits, careful not to let the two touch. I snagged a couple of biscuits and poured a glass of milk from the carafe left out on the counter. I pulled my usual chair out with my foot and dropped into it.

I munched casually through my breakfast. The eggs were a little dry, probably from sitting in the pan while Emma charged into my room dead set on apprehending our guest. Today's crossword puzzle sat in the center of the table with a blue line squiggled off one corner like she'd stopped in the middle of penning her answer, probably when she'd heard me talking to Clayton.

I paused to listen. *I wonder where that pesky Figment got to.* Around me the sounds of a tired old house creaked and groaned. As I swallowed the last mouthful of milk, footsteps, some quick and some slow, descended the stairs. Emma entered the kitchen, gaze darting fervently until she zeroed in on my place at the table. Clayton followed close on her heels with a crimson smear across his rapidly swelling bottom lip.

I gave Emma a quizzical look. She shrugged. "He had it coming."

"Yip! Yip! Yip!" High-pitched barks heralded Figment's return. She bounded in like a bunny through a field of clover, stopping to lick Emma's ankle.

I ignored the dog, which thankfully made no attempt to speak to me. My attention focused on Clayton instead. "Would you like some breakfast?" I pointedly looked at his split lip. "Or some ice to take the swelling down?"

He touched the sore spot, drawing away red-tinged fingers. "No thank you. I'm not hungry."

"In that case..." Emma smiled at Figment. By the time she looked back at Clayton, her bared teeth were gleaming. "Don't let the door hit you on the way out."

"Stop being rude."

She grumbled under her breath and stabbed a sausage fresh off the hotplate with her fork.

"It's all right. Emma has never made her feelings for me a secret."

Emma lifted the impaled link to her lips and snapped it cleanly in half. He didn't have to shudder. I did it for him. She chewed and skewered another piece. "And you've never made a secret of your feelings, either."

I clapped my hands loudly, bringing their attention back to me. I pointed at Emma, who ignored me in favor of the stove. "Stop the maneater routine and behave." She began heaping her plate with food. "This is my last day off this week and I would really like to get outside today. Are you sure you don't want to come?"

"I can't." She poured a glass of milk. "Someone has to go to work today. I'm dropping you off at the inn to spend your off day with Dana sans boyfriend. She has a spare room set up for you and everything."

I shook my head determinedly. I couldn't stand the thought of seeing Dana. Her saccharine sweetness turned my stomach at twenty paces. "I'm not going to the inn."

Emma carried her plate to the table and slammed it down over her placemat. "You can't stay out here alone. Think about it. We can't risk a repeat of what happened Tuesday."

Clayton crossed his arms over his chest as if preparing for battle. "I'll stay with her."

Hope stirred in me, but Emma crushed it flat.

"No, you will not. She will go to Dana's and like it. You're the last male she can trust herself to alone. I think you proved that last night."

I couldn't handle being the white elephant in the room any longer. I took the front doorknob in hand and turned towards my sister. "I love you, but you are not my mother. I respect that you want to keep me safe, but I am not spending the day with Dana unless it's shackled to the headboard."

I ignored the way Clayton's eyes darkened at my casual reference to bondage. I plucked at my shirt, sweltering under his stare. "I'm going to get some air."

"Stay on the porch," Emma yelled at my retreating back.

"Arrgghh!" I punched the screen door open and walked until the tips of my toes curled over the top porch step. Clayton stopped just behind me. Heat rolled off him in waves and broke against my back. I almost leaned into his warmth. I could tell he would have let me.

Clayton stepped aside and gave me room. "So I take it you don't like Dana."

"I didn't say that."

"No, you didn't have to say anything." I could hear the smile in his voice. When I didn't respond, his amusement waned. "You really don't like her, do you?"

"No, I really don't. I should like her. Everyone likes her.

She's never done or said anything out of line to me. She's just too perfect, too perky. It's not natural." The words tumbled out, having never been spoken. "You did ask."

"So I did." His broad-tipped fingers skimmed my arm. "What about me? Do you like me well enough to pass the day in my company?"

While I debated how wise it was to tell him exactly how much I liked him, I settled on a simple, "Yes." Then I spied my backpack slumped against the caned back of my rocking chair.

Clayton followed my line of sight. "I found it in the guard shack. I thought I'd return it while I was here."

"Thank you." I felt detached from the drama of two days past. Like it had happened to someone else or in one of those Lifetime movies Emma's always raving about.

"You mentioned wanting to go outside today. Did you mean Emasen or did you have something else in mind?"

I pointed down the snaking driveway where forest encroached on civilization and a wooded peak rose just far enough away you might have thought it was a mirage. "The mountain gives me the kind of peace I can't find anywhere else."

My means of obtaining that peace, I chose not to share. He had wings and would understand the rush of standing at the cliff's edge, feeling a breeze rise up to beckon you forward. He could answer the wind's call while I could only pretend.

"Is your leg up to it?"

I met his stormy eyes and challenged him. "It gets stronger every minute." I imitated Dana's southern-belle accent. "A big, strong male such as your sweet self shouldn't have any problem keeping up with a little ol' crippled demoness such as me." I hadn't meant to throw that last part in, but it was too late to take the words back now.

"You aren't crippled." He reached out, but let his hand fall back to his side. "You were brutalized. It doesn't change who you are."

"I know, I know, and I didn't mean to snap at you." I straightened my hair so the entire honey-blonde length fell down my back. "I'm just sensitive about it. If you're serious about taking me, then I'll go find a button-up to pull on."

"Are you cold?" His rough hands smoothed up and down my arms, wiping away the slight chill in the early morning air.

"Not really, but..." I stepped away from his warmth. "This top...it's tight and you can see...them."

"And you don't want me to?" His husky words thrilled me when they shouldn't have.

"Don't you not want to?"

His soft exhalation ended on a chuckle that seeped into my skin like pure sunshine, warming me to the tips of my bare toes. "Madelyn, you twist my head around until I don't know what I'm saying or doing around you."

"Sorry." My toes flicked away a paint chip from one of the weathered boards.

"Don't be. You're a complicated woman. I can appreciate that."

The *click, click, click* of nails on linoleum brought my attention back to the open front door. I smiled when I realized Clayton had left it open so Emma had a clear view of where we stood. Figment sat in the doorway, whining and flashing somber eyes at me.

"It's okay, I'm not mad," I said. "Feel free to go all Chatty Cathy on me."

The dog's tail wagged as she hopped up and trotted off to settle across Emma's feet like a pair of house slippers. She left without uttering a single word. I watched her go, baffled by her silence.

"Figment?" Clayton's cheeks dimpled. "Why do I think there's a story behind that?"

I lowered my voice to a bare whisper. "You try being chased through the woods by a khaki-clad nightmare only to be rescued by a talking fox." I looked back at Figment. "I thought I had gone crazy." She kept her face on her dainty paws, but her ears perked and leaned in our direction. "The jury is still out on that one, by the way."

"I didn't mean for you two to meet like that." He rubbed a hand across the nape of his neck. "I hadn't expected you two to meet at all."

"She was spying on me?" It would explain why our paths had crossed in the woods that night. "You asked her to follow me to the cemetery, didn't you?"

"No." He tucked his hands into his pockets, but still I saw them tighten into fists. "She did that on her own. She didn't tell me anything until she had you safely underground."

I chewed my bottom lip while digesting the fact that it seemed I owed her my life. "You always refer to her as she. What's her real name?"

"I've never called her anything. It's not my place."

"She's yours, how could you not name her?" I frowned. "What is she anyway?"

"She's an Aisling, a sentient being of light given into the keeping of one female in every Evanti generation."

I stated the obvious. "You aren't female."

"No," he said grimly. "When my mother died, the Aisling's name died with her. There were no females left to take Figment, so she came to me. She is the last of her kind."

A rush of pity filled me for the annoyingly endearing creature. It was hard being alone, an outcast and different from everyone else. "How did she know where to find me?"

He took the first step down. "Think about it. You're a half-Evanti female, the only surviving one I can name. By all rights, she should belong to you." He smiled. "You were the first person she's shown herself to in longer than I can remember." He paused on the second step. "Can you wait for a bit? I have to speak with Mason before I can leave."

"Sure," I said. "Take your time."

"Thanks." He waved to me and gave a high-pitched whistle, calling Figment outside. "Pack whatever supplies you'll need. I'll be back in an hour, two hours tops, and we'll take that hike."

I watched him settle behind the wheel of his Jeep. The engine roared into life and he drove away. I closed one eye and framed his fire-engine-red Wrangler between my thumb and finger. Pinching them closed, I opened them quickly. He was gone.

Chapter Eleven

The toes of my worn sneakers touched off the porch with every forward rock, kicking me back until momentum swept me downward. I pushed off again, rocked back, repeated.

"You're going to wear tracks in the porch if you don't stop soon." I glanced up as Emma pushed through the front door, pulling it closed behind her. Her lips puckered like she'd been sucking on a lemon. "Clayton said he would come, so he'll come." Bitterness laced her words. "He's nothing if not a male of his word." An angry tick worked in her cheek.

"What has he ever done to you?" I tugged the hem of her shirt to draw her attention from the road and down to me. "You're not usually one to hold a grudge."

She rested a hand on my shoulder. "He watched the person I love most suffer needlessly." Her grip tightened. "And he did nothing to stop it."

I stopped rocking. "Me? If anything could have been done to save either of us, any of us, Harper would have done it. He did do it. Clayton doesn't figure into the equation." Did he? What did I really know about the resentment simmering between Emma and Clayton? Less than nothing, that's what. "How could he have helped me? And when?"

Instead of answering, she tugged down her ponytail and offered me the hair band. "It looks like you'll need this more than I will today."

I was tired of being ignored, but her sullen expression stalled my brewing rant in its tracks. "What do you mean?" I finger combed my hair and wrapped the rubber band around it. The temptation to pull down the loose knot and allow my hair to cover my back was a nervous twitch in my hand.

Emma pointed down the road where a plume of red dust roared to life, chasing after a partially concealed vehicle. Clayton's topless Jeep came into sight just ahead of the cloud rolling up the driveway behind him. The tan hardtop was missing, leaving the cab exposed to delicious air currents.

"It's a pretty day to drive with the top down." I imagined driving fast enough would feel like flying. And why else would an Evanti drive a convertible? "This should be fun."

Emma didn't answer. She did take a half step closer to my chair.

The Jeep rolled to a stop in our yard's unofficial parking lot, a patch so worn grass gave up on growing there. Clayton unfolded long legs that carried him to where we waited on the porch. He tucked one hand in the front pocket of his pants while the other raked through the windblown tangle of black hair curling with sweat and sticking to his temples.

Serious eyes settled on me. "Are you ready to go?"

Emma pressed my shoulder down with her hand, refusing to let me rise. "Maybe I could stay home today. I could ask Marci or one of the others to cover my shift. They can't do the closing paperwork, but I could put in a few hours tonight after closing..."

"Emma." I patted the hand anchoring me in place. "I'll be fine. Clayton won't let anything happen to me." My gaze slid over to the towering male resting a lean, denim-clad hip against the porch's wooden rail. "Right?"

He waited the span of two heartbeats to reply. One longer than a simple "yes" should have taken. "I won't let anything happen to you. I promise."

"See?" I gave Emma's hand a final squeeze. "I'm in good hands."

She grumbled as I pried away her fingers. "That's what I'm afraid of."

"We'll be back in a couple of hours. Should I wait here for you or head to the diner?"

She passed over my backpack, which was stuffed with enough trail mix, water bottles and sunscreen to last a week in the Sahara rather than a few hours on a rock barely qualifying as a mountain. "Come to the diner. I have to start the closeout papers for the month and I don't want you left alone—period." Emma sighed, clearly unhappy. "We can eat there before heading home and save ourselves a few dishes."

"Okay." I stood and dropped a quick kiss on her cheek. "See you after awhile." I barely needed to guide my feet forward. Where Clayton was, I found myself wanting to be.

I forced myself to take slow, measured strides until I reached the porch's edge. He offered me a warm, firm hand to guide me down the steps, probably thinking pain caused the small tremors and shuffling gate.

The second our skin touched, my mind flashed back to his brother, and the night he'd escorted me to the edge of a grand ballroom, brimming with my mother's court and seething with eager anticipation. The chill dancing up my spine vibrated through our joined hands. I shook my head, divesting myself of the vision.

"Are you all right?" Clayton cupped his palm against the side of my throat, pausing with his thumb pressed against my pulse, measuring its frantic beats. "We can always do this another day."

Hope threaded his voice, but I needed fresh air and open spaces and had no qualms about using him to get them. "I'm fine, just getting my sea legs under me." I turned to Emma, wiggling fingers in a goodbye wave she didn't notice. Her eyes were locked on Clayton like a sniper with an easy target within range.

Angling my body between Emma's and Clayton's, I took the last two steps quickly, bumping into him in my hurry to separate the two. Even with both feet planted firmly on the ground, he kept possession of my hand, interlacing our fingers. Emma kept her eyes glued to that meeting of skin. I tried pulling away, but his grip only tightened.

"You can let go now."

His lips curved upward in a slow smile. "But I don't want to."

Using our joined hands, he tugged me along in his wake, evidently just as eager as I to escape Emma's gimlet glare. At the Jeep, he released his hold only long enough to open the passenger-side door before settling his hands at my waist.

"Hold on to me."

My arms circled his neck, linking at his nape and twisting in his hair. "You don't have to help me, you know. The seat isn't that far up."

Clayton ignored me. Digging his fingers into the soft flesh of my hips, he lifted me gently into my seat. His upper body following mine inside the Jeep's interior.

We stayed that way—Clayton bent over me, linked to me where my hands smoothed over the tense muscles bunching his shoulders. His hands were pinned between my body and the seat, but I wasn't foolish enough to think for a second I held the advantage.

The cab felt cramped and airless, too small and confining for the desires this male roused in me.

I didn't want to hold my breath and hope his gaze would seek mine. And when it happened, I didn't want my lips to telegraph their happiness with a smile, but they did.

Emma called from her station by the front door. "This is not what we agreed on." Her threat almost succeeded in dousing the fragile happiness igniting inside me. "You're taking her on a hike, not a date."

I don't know if he heard her and didn't care, or if he didn't hear and I didn't care, because he chose that moment to brush his soft lips over mine in a chaste kiss.

I wanted to blame pheromones or nature or circumstance for the wet rush of desire flooding my core, but I knew I would have wanted him the same no matter the time or place he'd found me. I pulled back, breaking the kiss and trembling anew because that knowledge frightened me. I had pined away five years of my life for another male, the brother of the demon whose essence lingered on my lips.

"You taste like citrus," I said stupidly.

His forehead braced against mine as he chuckled. "And you taste...addictive."

Our breaths mingled in a pleasant way.

"You did kiss me a lot last night." I couldn't help it sounding like an accusation.

His nose bumped mine. "Good-night kisses."

"And now? What sort of kiss was that?"

"I forgot to kiss you good morning." His lips covered mine again. "I was...distracted."

Blood flushed my cheeks, making his Jeep's paint job pale by comparison. So much for pretending he hadn't seen me naked. I groaned. "Don't remind me."

"I'll remember enough for the both of us," he teased, dimples deeper than I'd ever seen them. "You're beautiful. All of you."

I rested a hand on the soft fabric over his chest. His heart hammered against his rib cage. "I don't know how to do this, how to be with you this way."

Whatever he might have said was overshadowed by Emma grabbing his leather belt. "Back off," she said, using the belt to haul Clayton backwards out of the Jeep.

Emma slammed the door shut hard enough to make me jump. Her gaze pinned Clayton to the spot. "Don't make me regret entrusting her to your care."

The muscles in his jaw worked, but he bit back whatever words he might have spoken with obvious effort. His eyes met mine, and I had no doubt his attempt at civility was for my sake.

Her hard eyes turned on me. "Be safe. Remember what I taught you." Her gaze wandered back to Clayton. "If you have to put him down, make sure he doesn't get back up."

Clayton turned his back on her and stalked towards the Jeep. I scooted until the door cut into my side, as far away from his anger as I could get, which only incensed him further. "You don't have to be scared of me. I won't let myself hurt you."

I nodded at his far-from-soothing words. They implied he could hurt me. That he had definitely thought about it, or the possibility of it. I swallowed the anxious lump rising in my throat.

Clayton's head dropped against his seatback, eyes closed, and he inhaled sharply before pushing out a slow exhale, as if cooling his temper. He repeated the process a few times, tilting his face carefully away from me.

Then I understood. The topless ride, his short temper and his failing attempts to curb it. They conveyed his struggle against my pheromonal calling card.

The day was clear and cool, probably cooler than warranted the top being removed. Clayton didn't want to be trapped with my scent. I sniffed discreetly, but smelled only the spice of his cologne and the Jeep's new-car smell.

"Are you sure you're okay to do this?" My hesitancy brought his head up.

"I'm fine." He twisted the key and the Jeep rumbled to life. He threw it in gear and sped away from where my sister sat on the lowest porch step, holding her head in her hands. I touched the side-view mirror with my finger, stroking her cascade of golden ringlets through the reflection and leaving a smudge behind.

"You're being quiet." Wind whistled past my ears, making him raise his voice to be heard over the road noise.

"I don't really have anything to say." I picked at the zipper on my backpack, half tempted to pop in ear buds, switch on my iPod and avoid the uncomfortable conversation he'd started. "What about you? You're not saying much."

His fingers tightened on the wheel. "I'm thinking. That's all."

"Can I ask you something?"

A moment passed. "Yes."

"If you want to be with me, then I have to ask about Dana."

When his eyes met mine, they flickered darkly. "Do you really want to know?"

Ordinarily, I wouldn't have pushed, but this mattered to me. It should have mattered to him. "I have to know if you have some sort of relationship with her. The children—"

"Look exactly like their father." His teeth snapped together hard. "Do you want to know who their sire is?" When I didn't answer, he snorted derisively. "I didn't think so. No one really wants to know. They're too happy whispering behind my back to ask for the truth."

"Dana has done everything but screen-print paternity T-shirts with your face on them. If it's not true, then you should set the record straight." A loose strand of hair whipped around my face, forcing me to catch it and tuck it back in place. "Jacob told me the children were Harper's."

Clayton's eyes darkened still, filling with anguish. "This isn't about me at all, is it?" He slammed his palms against the wheel. "This is about whether or not Saint Harper jumped the fence during his visits to the colony."

I shifted in my seat, turning my back to him. "That was cruel, and I didn't deserve it. Neither did your brother." Drawing my knees up to my chest, I rested them against my door and fished my iPod from the backpack's front pouch, uncoiling the tiny earphones and tucking them into my ears.

Heavy metal bouncing inside my head drowned out any possibility for talk. He might have called my name, but I acted like I hadn't heard. We drove through the suburbs occupied by colonists, then through the more human-rich areas until we were caught by the single red light strung across the town's only major intersection.

On the street corner, a small assembly of the colony wives stood, waiting to cross as they cuddled newborns or bounced toddlers on their hips. Some clutched bags from the day's shopping excursion, while others held chubby hands.

While stopped, I took the chance to swap out ear buds, having forgotten about the frayed end of cord attached to my favorite pair. I rooted through the deeper pockets of my bag, searching for the unopened set I'd bought earlier in the week.

Lynn, one of the cooks employed by my sister, paused and tugged on her friend's sleeve. "Do you see that? Madelyn is in the Jeep with Clayton." Her friend's neck craned for a better look. "I wonder if Dana knows."

The friend clicked her tongue slowly. "He probably feels sorry for her." The woman bent down to retrieve her bags from the sidewalk. "I heard she's deformed or something. It's why she never leaves her house. None of the males want anything to do with her." Bags in hand, she lobbed her parting shot. "She's just some hoity-toity princess, too good to socialize with the rest of us. You'd think that apron she wears every day would clue her in on the fact she's not royalty any longer."

Lynn shared in the laugh that followed as they crossed the street. She would have to be blind not to realize the top was down and that I'd heard their every word. Tears pricked my eyes, but I wouldn't let them see me cry. Maybe once Clayton drove off, I could blame them on windburn.

I jumped when his hand landed on my shoulder, startled by the unexpected contact. When I glanced at him, his eyes were soft and troubled. Great, he'd heard the women too.

I didn't want to hear his two cents, so I tapped my earphones and held up the iPod, hoping he would take the hint. He nodded and looked both ways to make certain the last of the women and children had crossed before reaching over to swipe away a tear I hadn't noticed falling down my cheek. Illusion ruined, I unplugged and curled up tighter in my seat until my chin stabbed the top of the knee it rested on.

The Jeep lurched as Clayton accelerated, leaving behind what had happened. All the hustle and bustle of town melted to serene, peaceful forest. Foliage became denser, darker. Nothing but sky and air remained this far outside the city limits.

Out here, I could breathe.

Clayton braked at the junction of a small fork in the road. "Is there a trail you prefer?"

I pointed towards a sign labeled "The Emasen Bluff Pass".

Taking the gently sloped path winding around the mountain's base, we circled into a clearing leveled with gravel and marked as an RV camping site. He parked and I opened my own door, stepping out before he could reach me.

With knees straight, I bent down to touch my toes and hung there, pulling my leg muscles taut before beginning a few rudimentary stretches and working the kinks from my back. When I straightened, Clayton leaned against the Jeep, arms crossed, watching me with interest. My backpack dangled from his fingers.

I closed the space between us. He held out the pack and helped me shrug into it. I looked towards the mouth of the trail. "Are you coming?"

His hand sought mine and meshed our fingers together in silent apology. I couldn't hold on to my anger while his thumb rubbed gentle circles over my skin. I resisted the urge to smile as we passed a wooden trail marker spray painted with the words "Happy Hiking".

Two steps up the path a blur of red fur whizzed past my ear. Tiny, needlelike claws dug into my skin as whatever it was skidded to a halt across my shoulders.

I screamed and threw my pack to the ground, running farther up the trail while swatting my neck and back and shoulders. The tiny animal scurried over my body unhindered by gravity, making my skin crawl everywhere it touched. "Clayton, help me!" Continuing to jump and shake, stomp and squirm, I tried to rid myself of the rodent.

"What kind of game is this?"

I stopped screaming and forced myself to look down where a red squirrel hung from my pants leg. "Figment?"

"Yes?"

I stumbled backwards until I bumped into a sapling tree. "You just scared ten years off my life."

"Oh, I'm so sorry. I didn't know you could do that."

"What?" I forced myself to hold still while she climbed to a higher, more secure location. "No, not literally, I just mean that you scared me very badly."

"Are you all right?" Clayton asked.

"Yes, just surprised is all." I glanced at the furball sitting on my shoulder. "I think I liked it better when she was a fox."

The russet squirrel hiked up my side, gripping my hair with one of her furry hands as she leaned out and wiggled squirrelly fingers at him. I felt oddly flattered by the gesture she emulated.

Shock didn't begin to cover how I'd felt after being assaulted by a flying squirrel, but Clayton didn't look surprised. In fact, he looked relieved. "Thank you for coming."

Figment chattered happily. *"You are most welcome."* She sailed from her perch, gliding over to Clayton and landing spread-eagle across his abdomen before scurrying up to nestle against his neck. He scratched her tiny head, something I had never thought to do, and she purred as she had for Emma.

This was exactly why I didn't need a pet. I didn't know how to work one properly.

"Well," I said, straightening my clothes. "Now that the gang's all here, we best get started. I'd like to reach the top before it gets much later."

Clayton hooked a finger through the belt loop of my jeans. "Lead the way."

Figment leapt from his shoulder and scurried back up into

the trees. I watched her zigzag from limb to limb until my eyes crossed. "Man, she has some serious energy."

He gave my pants a tug. "Light is radiant energy."

I snorted. "Smart ass, that's not what I meant and you know it."

We continued to ascend until the twinge in my knee became more of a sharp pang. My steps lagged and he, of course, noticed.

"Is your leg bothering you?"

I tried to brush off his concern. "It's nothing. I guess my knee got mangled worse than I thought. I should have been over this by now."

He grabbed the pack from my shoulder and dropped it to the ground. "Let's take a break." He looked up at the bright blue sky. "We still have plenty of daylight left to spend up here, so there's no reason to push so hard."

"Fine." I huffed as I lowered myself to the ground. Clayton took a seat beside me and angled so that he faced the trailhead while I faced the trail itself. He draped my sore leg across his lap and made small circular frictions around the side of the knee joint, starting from the front of the patella and working around.

My head dropped back. "That feels unbelievably good."

I felt his laughter beneath my leg. "I like making you feel good."

I smiled, eyes closing. "So I've noticed."

His massage took an upward turn, his hands journeying until his fingertips almost brushed the juncture of my thighs.

My cheeks burned while I tried to act indifferent to his touch. I mean, accidents do happen. I relaxed under his gentle pressure while he worked out the worst of the pain. Then it happened again. His thumb stroked along the thick denim seam running between my legs.

I lifted my head slowly, squeezing my legs together as I sat more upright. Clayton centered his attention where I'd trapped his large hand.

"Tell me to stop," he whispered.

I forced myself to relax as the now-familiar flush of desire rose in me. "What if I don't want you to?" His concern made me question his control, but I wasn't afraid. I was captivated, drawn into the depth of his gaze.

Then a rain of pinecones pelted his back and my arms. I brushed away the dirt and thorny barbs.

"Look what I've found!" Figment scrabbled across the worn path, tossing and head butting the dried-out husks of pinecones, mostly picked apart by real squirrels seeking the seed inside the prickly shell.

"That's great." Disappointment at being interrupted settled around me. I tried not to focus on the dull ache between my legs. We were being watched, so I tried to convince myself that rolling my hips into his hand was a bad idea.

A final glance at Figment's inquisitive assessment of what parts went where gave me the strength I needed to pull away. "Just wonderful."

Clayton stood and tugged me to my feet, helping me into my backpack.

He glanced up, his face impassive as Figment scampered up to his shoulder. "You can go ahead. We'll let you enjoy your solitude." Clayton continued to rub her ears. "Just don't go too far."

"Yeah, okay." I resumed my hike, leaving as the pair whispered to one another, shutting me out of their conversation. Shoulders back, I pressed on alone. If they didn't want to play with me, then I didn't want to play with them. Maturity, thy name is Madelyn.

Pushing up the trail harder than I should have, I almost missed the turn guiding me up the final incline to where the landscape dropped away before me. Trees and rocks jutted up off to my left and right, but ahead lay nothing. My legs ached from the effort of climbing to Emasen's cliff edge, but the view made the burn worthwhile.

Exhausted, I shrugged out of my backpack, letting it slide down my arms to land with a soft thud on the compacted earth. Sweat stung my eyes. Perspiration beaded on my skin, struggling to squeeze through the coating of waterproof sunscreen Emma had made me apply before allowing me to leave the house.

I walked to the edge of the precipice and stood with the toes of my sneakers hanging over the sheer rock face of the cliff. My shoulders tensed, air whooshed into my lungs as I rolled to the balls of my feet, preparing for the impossibility of flight.

"Step back from the ledge," Clayton's soft voice coaxed from behind me.

"Clayton," I groaned. "I wasn't really going to jump." I pointed towards my back. "No wings, remember?" As if either of us could forget.

I twisted abruptly, discounting the lingering tenderness in my knee, and lost my footing. Arms flailing, I tried to regain my balance and failed, toppling backwards from the ledge.

"Clayton!" I shouted his name as my body whistled through the air, plummeting towards the earth. Frantic heartbeats thundered in my ears, drowning out the sound of my screams.

As I fell, my earliest memories flickered through my mind. I pushed aside the barrage of images and settled on my favorite.

That of a black-skinned boy with glittering onyx eyes. And wings. Tiny, ruby-red wings that had fluttered with his excitement and made my child's heart long for the half of my heritage I lacked.

"Madelyn!" Clayton bellowed, leaping from the edge and following me into the sky.

I had only a fraction of a second to wonder if he would make it before his strong arms plucked me from my downward spiral.

His enormous scarlet wings opened wide, stretching out so far in either direction I couldn't see the blackened tips and tiny, hook-like hands that topped them.

Clayton's blunt chin dug into the top of my head. The muscular arms holding me close tightened until my breath wheezed from my lungs.

"Were you trying to get yourself killed?" he snapped. "What if I hadn't been there? What if you'd been alone?" His skin trembled beneath my fingers.

"It was an accident." I struggled in his hold, trying to free my arms from where he pinned them to my sides. "If you hadn't startled me, I wouldn't have fallen in the first place."

"You can't be so careless." He held me dangling in the air before him, shaking me senseless, before tucking me back against his chest. His voice cracked. "What would I have done without you?" His thumb worked across a bony protrusion behind my shoulder blade, marking my absence of wings.

"It's okay, really." I rested my cheek against his chest since my hands weren't free. "A fall from that height would have hurt." I carefully avoided making a comment on my personal experiences. "But I would have healed eventually."

"I don't want to hear this." His head tossed from side to side. "I don't want to know how you know that."

If I'd thought he couldn't hold me tighter, I'd been wrong. I would wear bruises for a while, but for now, I allowed him to have what he needed, letting him squeeze until joints popped and pain blossomed. It was such a small hurt when compared to the anguish carried in his voice.

Using my chin to part the fabric of his shirt, I rested my face flush against his skin. His body shuddered beneath my cheek. His desperate groan filled my ear with his heated breath as he glided the last few feet and touched down.

Still gripping my upper arms, Clayton lowered me to the ground, sliding me down his body so slowly time felt suspended. With earth beneath my feet, I leaned into him, trying to calm his ragged nerves. Something hard pressed against my stomach, making me shift to get comfortable and him growl low in his throat. Oh. *Oh.*

"Madelyn..." His voice grew husky.

I pulled back, meeting his gaze. "You really are worked up over this." I twisted in a circle before him. "I'm fine. See?"

"Madelyn..."

"Don't beat yourself up over it." I touched his arm, the muscle beneath my hand pulled taut as a bowstring.

"Run," he grated out over his lips.

I spun around, searching for another demon or a wild animal, unable to imagine anything Clayton couldn't protect me against. We were alone in the ravine. No one or thing had followed us here. "Why? What's wrong?"

Our eyes locked. I gasped and backed away slowly. Clayton's pupils flashed silver, huge, luminous, and spellbinding. His wings twitched with his effort to still them, but vibrant reds saturated his skin as his arousal heightened and called forth my body's own response.

"Go." He clutched his head, breaths ragged. "Run!"

I turned, but from the corner of my eye I saw him fall to the ground. Instead of leaving, I took a half step forward.

"Get away from me!" He slashed the air inches from my face with razor-tipped claws. "I can't control myself. It's too much. Your scent..." His wings stretched and then cloaked his body as he hid himself from me. "Find Figment, she knows the way."

This time he didn't have to ask twice. I spun on my heel and ran. Rocks turned my ankles and bramble tugged on my pants legs as I covered the familiar ground. I don't know how he expected me to find Figment. I hadn't seen her since she'd ditched me for Clayton earlier, and there was no time to look for her now. I had to run.

To my right a narrow trail hugged the mountainside, leading up and away from the basin and the tormented demon rocking on his heels beneath the shelter of his wings. I took a step towards the upward path.

"Not that way. He'll see you."

I jerked my head around in time to see Figment glide from her tree-side hideout onto my shoulder, which quivered with the need to shake her loose. Her small chest heaved from exertion. She must have raced us to reach the bottom. "Up is the only way out. The ravine is a dead end on both sides."

"There's a crevice at the base of the mountain. Follow it through to the other side. He can't reach you from the air if you stay inside the mountain."

Using her tiny paw, she pushed my cheek to the left and I saw it. The locals called it a fat-man squeeze, but I hadn't realized it ran the length of the mountain. A fissure in the rock face made an uncovered chute where an aerial scout could see me, but the depth of the trail carved into the rock would guard from an overhead attack.

A tortured cry rose behind me, reverberating through the rocky basin. This could not be happening. Not again. But here I was, legs burning as I ran for the shelter of the crevice and slipped inside. Jagged rocks scraped my hips and hands as I felt my way through the opening and entered the chute. Graffiti covered the walls where the local teens had claimed the space as their own.

Bracing along the smoother rocks, I used them to keep my balance as I hustled through a larger space, just wide enough for two people to fit side by side. I heard the crunch of cardboard flatten beneath my heel and looked down. A box stuck to my shoe and when I finally managed to scuff it off, I was rewarded by the Trojan logo smiling up at me.

"Eww." I wiped my hands on my jeans. "Just eww." Damn teenagers and their lack of hygiene.

A shadow fell across me, darkening the broader alley. I knew, but couldn't stop myself from looking up. Clayton was suspended in the air above me. His eyes were wide and unseeing. His chest heaved as his fingers flexed open and closed at his sides, waiting for a chance to put them to use.

I glanced at Figment still clinging to my shoulder. Her beady eyes stared up at him, disbelieving, which did nothing for my confidence.

"What do we do now? He's going to wait us out or catch us on the other side."

"Keep going." She ran a paw over my hair. *"I'll distract him and you run for the Jeep."*

"No, Fig—" I tried to catch her, but she was gone, scampering over the rocky outcroppings until she cleared the gap. She soared into the air, landing on Clayton's face and sinking claws into either cheek while using her body as a blindfold.

"Run. I can't hold him for long."

"I can't just leave you."

"Please, for both our sakes, you must keep yourself safe."

"Fine, but if he hurts one hair on your head, then when this is over, his ass is grass."

Scrambling over the uneven rocks, I made my escape. A sliver of daylight grew until I burst through it, out the other side, and into the campground. The Jeep sat alone in the empty lot, salvation within easy reach. Gravel crunched beneath my feet, bogging me down when I needed speed.

I skidded around the driver's side, yanking the door open and hauling myself inside before tugging the door shut with a solid *whack*. Keys glinted in the ignition.

In an instant I realized he'd known this would happen. Why else would he have left the keys? And Figment. He'd even brought along a chaperone. As the flood of clues I should have noticed compounded, I felt doubly the fool. I'd known he struggled against his desire for me, and still I had made him bring me here to this isolated spot where I'd further baited him with kisses.

With a harsh twist of my wrist, the engine turned over and cranked. Spinning wheels and spraying gravel, I sped towards the trail leading to the highway. My foot couldn't press the pedal down hard enough. The engine thrummed, vibrating through a rough patch until the road turned smooth.

I drove, hard and fast, watching the road while casting glances in the rearview mirror. With the top gone, he could reach in and pluck me from my seat. Not a happy thought.

The hairs on my neck prickled as if dozens of tiny spiders paraded across my nape. I looked up to see Clayton gliding overhead, thrusting his wings to pull ahead of the speeding Jeep. I stomped the gas pedal to the floorboard. He sailed past me, gaining a few car lengths before he stopped and hovered in the center of my lane with outstretched arms.

I slammed on the brakes, knowing it was too late to stop. Tires spinning, the Jeep swung sideways as the grill smashed into Clayton's hips with a shattering crunch.

His body flew backwards, tumbling over asphalt until he rolled to a stop on his back with one wing twisted beneath him and the other twitching and broken beside him.

"Clayton!" I leapt over the half door. My feet smacked the pavement as I ran to him. Dropping to the ground, I lightly touched his shoulder. He winced and half-opened hazy blue-gray eyes.

"You idiot. I could have killed you!"

His chest rattled on his next indrawn breath. "I would have hurt you."

"You wouldn't have hurt me." I didn't know where the certainty came from, but I didn't question it. I stroked my fingers across his ruined cheek. "Clayton—"

"Shh." He pressed a kiss into my palm. "It's my fault." His eyes drifted closed. "Always you, Maddie. Always." Then he went still.

I shook his arm, but he didn't move again or speak. I shoved from the ground and ran to the Jeep, searching under the seats and in the console, finally finding what I sought in the glove box. A cherry red cell phone, an exact replica of the one Figment had produced that morning in my bedroom.

My knee-jerk response was to call Emma, but I didn't trust her not to make things worse. I swallowed, tasting my pride slide down my throat like sandpaper, and punched in Dana's number instead.

"Hello?"

"You're home."

"Of course I am, silly. Parker is home from school because of swelling in his leg. I think the cast is too tight." Water ran in the background. "Did you need something?"

I stared at the hulking mass of demon sprawled in a crumpled heap across the road. "You have to help me." I tamped down my fear and tried to steady my voice. "Clayton took me on a hike." Her silence told me she hadn't known. "Something happened and I...I ran over him."

"You *what*?" I heard something break, like maybe she'd been doing dishes when I called and now had one less to dry. "You mean with a *car*?"

"It was his Jeep." Hysteria was creeping up on me. "Look, he's passed out and I need help to move him. Please help me."

"Calm down," she snapped. "Where are you?"

Peering through the windshield, I noted a metal sign a few yards ahead. "We're at mile marker twenty-nine, just before you reach Emasen."

"Don't try to move him. I'll get help and meet you there." The line died.

I tossed the phone in the passenger seat and walked back to Clayton, dropping to the pavement. He lay so still. I took his hand in mine and held tight, brushing a curl from across his forehead.

"Stupid, stubborn, male. You didn't have to do this. I would have survived anything you could have done to me." I stroked his bruised cheek with the backs of my fingers and smoothed over his busted lips with my thumb. "You have to be okay. I can't lose you too."

Regrets weighted my conscious. Even when I heard the distant hum of engines, I couldn't lift my head. I slumped there, holding his hand, forcing his fingers to mesh with mine, and felt my heart fragment. Brakes caught and tires squealed over blacktop. Two sets of doors opened, one shut. And I still couldn't look up.

I almost believed if I took my eyes from Clayton that he would leave me, and I couldn't go through that again. I'd just begun to live, to think beyond today and look forward to waking in the morning. I couldn't lose him. I wasn't strong enough.

"Clayton." Dana's high-pitched cries succeeded in snapping my head up. "What has she done to you?" She shoved me aside, breaking my connection with his hand so she could kneel where I had knelt, checking his pulse before turning on me. "How could you do this to him?"

"It was an accident. I didn't mean for him to get hurt."

She looked over my shoulder. "Why were you driving his Jeep? Why was he chasing you?" Her eyes narrowed. "He tried to claim you, didn't he?"

"No. Maybe? I—I don't know what happened. We were hiking. I fell, and when he caught me, he went crazy and told me to run so I did."

Dana's shoulders hunched over Clayton. "You could have killed him. Maybe Jacob wasn't in the wrong. Maybe it's been you the whole time."

One of the males she'd brought for backup, Mason I think his name was, spoke up. "You don't mean that. Madelyn wouldn't hurt a fly and you know it. This is all a misunderstanding. Clayton will set the record straight when he wakes up."

"If he wakes up," she sniffed, dabbing her fingertips under her eyes.

Mason waved to another, taller male to step forward. Together, they lifted Clayton and carried him to the rear of

165

Dana's truck. She lowered the tailgate, and blankets spilled out from where she'd lined the bed of the truck in preparation for his transport. The Evans Inn logo flashed in black relief on the topmost comforter, leaving me no doubt of his destination.

Making my way back to the Jeep, I crawled inside and shifted into gear, then followed the speeding trucks back to the inn.

Chapter Twelve

I drummed my fingers in slow succession across the steering wheel. There wasn't a single vacant parking space left at Evans Inn. Dana must have reached out and touched every branch of the colony's phone tree to have the lot filled so quickly. The overflow of vehicles hugged either side of the road, forcing the oncoming traffic to straddle the dotted line in turns to fit through the narrow gap.

Peering through the windshield, I spotted a stretch of curb large enough to accommodate the Jeep. As luck would have it, the only open space shared the diner's side of the street. I sat close enough to smell today's special and have my stomach rumble in response.

My feet itched to hit pavement, torn between running to Emma and going to Clayton. The temptation to tell my sister what I'd done and leave her to fix my mistakes tightened my fingers on the door handle. I hated that weakness in me. Relaxing my hold on the lever, I slipped my hand into my lap.

I cared for Clayton. I had been the one to hurt him and I would be the one to face him. I could understand Harper's insistence that he clean up his own messes now, and respected his memory more for knowing he'd done the right thing no matter the cost. I would follow his example.

"Aren't you going in?"

I started to find Figment, back on four legs and collared, sitting in the bucket seat beside me.

"Hey, I was worried about you."

"Clayton sent me away." Her fey voice sounded lost.

I twisted to face her. "Can't you, I don't know, pop in to see him?" Whatever the source of her magic, it clearly didn't suffer the limitations of anything I'd encountered.

"I promised him I would stay with you." Streaks of wet fur slicked to her cheeks. I didn't think dogs could cry, but what did I know?

I scratched behind her silky ears and she leaned into my hand. Maybe Emma was on to something with this pet thing after all. Any other time, this contact would have felt nice.

A horn honked behind me as traffic started to back up. "Come on, girl. Let's go see Clayton."

Her tail thumped against the seat, and when I opened my door, she was the first thing through it. When I joined her on the concrete, her trotting gate forced me to jog to keep up. We reached the crosswalk before I realized we were being watched.

Standing to either side of the inn's door were the males I'd seen earlier. The ones who had come with Dana to fetch Clayton.

Mason stood bulky and blond, blue-eyed with a grin creasing well-worn laugh lines. The male to his right was taller, leaner and less familiar. I crossed over to them.

Mason tipped his head. "Miss Madelyn, I don't know that you'll want to head in there just now. Dana has the women frothed up over Clayton's condition."

His partner's gaze traveled over me. He didn't look interested as much as irritated. "He's right. She's organizing a witch hunt and I'm afraid you're the one left holding the pointed hat."

I met the man's quiet eyes. They were cold, and one didn't match the other. Arctic blue clashed with vibrant green. A long scar began on his forehead, crossing over his nose and through his right eye to emerge at his temple before vanishing beneath his shaggy chestnut hair.

"I have to see Clayton."

"You shouldn't be left alone with any male until the next forty-eight hours have passed. You'll have plenty of time to talk later."

My ears burned with embarrassment. Figment pressed against my ankle. "You're counting down the days?" Had everyone known about my cycle but me?

The male's bicolored eyes crinkled at the corners, and I had the feeling that didn't happen often. "We were trained to know, sweet."

"Dillon." The single word rang with warning.

My pulse kicked up a notch.

And Dillon knew it, too, because he smiled before continuing. "Your mother felt certain slave's talents lied in areas beyond guarding a lady's chamber door. Even First Court ladies have itches in need of scratching." His fingernails lengthened and darkened. "And I found they liked my claws just fine."

Figment snarled, moving to position herself between Dillon and me.

"That's enough." Mason's glare said plenty.

Dillon leaned back against the inn's siding. Speaking to no one in particular, he said, "She should move along now. Not that I don't appreciate her *bouquet*, but I would like to avoid Clayton killing me for doing what I've been trained to do."

Mason frowned at the male before turning his attention

back to me. "He's right. If you have to see Clayton, make it fast and then get the hell away from any males you're not looking to claim." He ran a hand through his unkempt hair. "It's nice seeing you like this. Like someone reached in and turned all the lights on. It looks good on you." His cheeks pinked.

Mine did too. "Thanks." I stepped forward. "Excuse me."

I passed between them and entered the lobby with Figment close on my heels.

The inn's interior was classic country bed-and-breakfast with rich reds and gold covering the walls and floor. Comfortable, overstuffed furniture filled out the space. The cloying scent of potpourri hung heavy in the air, fighting it out and winning over the individual fragrances worn by the women milling around the room.

It was like I had walked in on a town meeting no one had seen fit to invite me to. Not that the old Maddie would have come. The males were right to warn me. All Dana needed was a bonfire and pitchforks because she had stoked the anger and indignation in the room to a fevered high. Mob mentality seldom worked out well for the target of all that pent-up confusion, and I could almost feel the bull's-eye painted on my chest.

Dana stood with her back to me and addressed the room. "I've never seen anything so, so brutal." She sniffled. "Madelyn just stood there, looking at Clayton like he was dirt on the bottom of her shoe. If the boys and I hadn't happened to drive by, why, she might have left him out there to die alone." Then she hammered the nails into my proverbial coffin. "She's Askaran. What's one more Evanti life to her kind?"

My fingers pinched the heavy seams of my jeans to keep me from snatching every perfectly coiffed hair from her head. Conversation ebbed as I reached Dana. I wanted to clean out my ears because I could not have heard her correctly. She glanced over her shoulder, caught sight of me and glared. Her next words, however, I heard just fine.

"You have a lot of nerve showing up here after what you've done."

"I came to see Clayton." Several faces scrunched up as if suddenly smelling something foul. Belatedly I realized the "something" was me. Obviously, I didn't hold the same appeal in mated circles as I did among the unmated. That was good to know.

"Haven't you done enough damage?" Dana crossed her twiggy arms across her thin chest. "I won't let you upset him when he needs to rest."

"I never meant to hurt him. You know what really happened. It was an accident."

Her flushed cheeks darkened with embarrassment she was quick to cover. "What I know is that we all helped keep Clayton's secret. We all wanted what was best for you, and this is how you repay us? Attacking our leader? His protection keeps our homes and families safe from your kind."

She addressed the room. "You know what I think? I think she couldn't stand looking in Clayton's face and seeing the likeness of his brother. I think she wanted him dead too, because he looks like her precious Harper."

I took a step closer. She took a step back.

"You met him three days ago." She made her case before the others. "And today you almost killed him. That can't be a coincidence."

"Are you accusing me of something?" Dana was no Evanti, and in my hands her brittle human bones would break.

A throaty growl rumbling from down the hall ended our standoff.

"Let her come," Clayton said.

And I answered, "Let them try to stop me."

His words were my assurance. As I spun towards the sound, Dana's grasping hands slid over my arm without purchase. Her location became distant and unimportant to me as I broke into the short hall leading to the first-floor suites.

Shrouded in darkness, a single shaft of light filtered through the narrow crack of a door left ajar. My palm rested on the satiny oak-stained panel for a second before I pushed inside.

Clayton sat upright on the bed's edge with his beautiful wings draped across his shoulders at rest. When he looked up, they flushed from carmine to scarlet, and he used glamour to conceal them from me. His shirt was gone, baring smooth skin bandaged with darkly tinted gauze. Pain emanated from him, so intense I took a step back before he thought to conceal that too.

"I didn't expect to see you so soon." His gaze roved over the ceiling, not seeing me at all.

"I was worried about you." I stepped just inside his room.

"Leave the door open," he said, and I did. "You shouldn't have come. It's not safe for you to be alone with me."

"We're not alone," I reasoned with him. "There are dozens of colonists in the den and guards posted at the front door." I pointed to the bed. "We still have our chaperone." Figment lay pressed firmly against his thigh, her eyes blissfully closed and at peace by her master's side.

He relaxed. "Good. That's good." His arms opened and I went into them, bracing my palms on the tops of his thighs and kneeling between his widespread legs.

He sat unmoving as I leaned my face against his bare chest and wrapped my arms around to where tension coiled low in his back. His muscles tautened beneath my fingers while mine went lax. Relief surged through me, and something more. Sheltered by this male's body, I felt safe, protected. I felt like I'd come home.

"What happened out there?" I pressed the words into his skin.

"I succumbed." His cheek came to rest atop my head. "I thought I could resist the call to mate, but I couldn't." He swallowed, dropping his hands to fist in the covers at his sides. "When you fell and your heart was racing, your body pressed against mine." A shiver coursed through him. "I couldn't resist." Fabric tore. "I didn't want to resist."

I felt him tense and shift. "It's okay," I said as he gripped my upper arms gently. "It was my fault. I could tell you didn't want to go, but I made you take me anyway." He set me aside as he stood. "I've gone about this all wrong. Let me make it up to you."

He ignored my concern and angled his chin towards the door. "I'm sorry you had to deal with Dana. She's not usually so rabid, even where I'm involved."

I pushed to my feet too. Looking so far up to Clayton put a crick in my neck. "It's okay. She cares about you and she doesn't like the idea of competition."

"Damn it, she's a friend, nothing more. I've tried to help her. I felt sorry for her, but after the way she treated you, even that label no longer applies."

I shouldn't have asked, but I blurted it out anyway. "Has she always been...just a friend?"

His eyes blackened. "Yes, she has never been more than a friend to me." They shimmered into sterling awareness. "There has never been anyone for me but you."

My hand raised to my throat, then slid lower to cover my

heart, grateful for the cage confining it. "But you stayed away. Because Harper loved me?"

Clayton's dry laughter was harsh, but self-directed. "I stayed away because you loved him. If I had only to risk my brother's happiness..." His voice trailed off.

I couldn't believe him. A male like Clayton wouldn't have waited...how long *had* he waited? "I don't know what to say."

"I don't expect you to say anything." He lifted a hand to quiet me. "You're the next best thing to my brother's widow. I have no right, no reason to hope you would claim me." His hand dropped. "Please, just leave. I don't want you to see me like this."

"I—"

He lashed out, knocking a vase filled with flowers to the floor. Glass shattered and flowers rolled free of the wreckage. "You don't owe me anything. God knows you don't owe me any kindness. Not after what I've done to you. What I want to do to you." He walked to the far corner of his room, turning his back on me. "Take Figment with you. You'll need protection for the last two days of your cycle."

So he was counting down the time too. I blinked back tears. "No, I'd rather she stayed with you. I'll go to Emma. She'll take care of me." Like always. "Can I see you again? When this is over?"

He nodded once, sharply. He braced his forearm against the wall and leaned into it while he waited for me to leave. I backed out of his room and bumped right into Dana.

"Leaving so soon?" She slammed the door closed in my face.

I didn't answer, just turned to leave when she grabbed my torn shirtsleeve. I glanced down at her hand and she released the fabric.

"I just thought you might want to know Jacob was released from custody today." She looked thoughtful. "Something about the mix of pheromones and caffeine impairing his judgment kept them from pressing charges."

My fingers trembled, so I shoved them into my pockets. "Clayton—"

"Doesn't know and won't know until he's recovered." She smiled and wiggled her fingers in a mocking wave. "Drive safely now."

She slipped past me, cracking the door open and slinking inside Clayton's bedroom. I almost reached out, but kept my hand at my side. He said there was nothing between them and I believed him. Whatever Dana's game, it would end now, and I didn't have to be here to witness it. I trusted the male and his word completely.

As I started down the hall, the big picture of my life blurred around the edges, refusing to let me call the image's entirety into focus. Understanding eluded me while questions left simmering in my mind reached the boiling point. Clayton had exhausted the supply of answers he was willing to give, but I knew where to find more.

As I made my way through the den, the women shuffled aside to let me pass. The few males present kept their bodies between their wives and me. A few looked interested. A few more looked worried, but whether for me or Clayton I wasn't sure. I felt the weight of their stares on my back as I pulled the front door open.

Crossing the threshold, I realized my mistake. It was dark and I was trapped. The visit with Clayton, coupled with Dana's interference as I came and went meant I was leaving later than planned. And wasn't that a happy accident? I would have to call Emma to come for me, which wouldn't be pretty since I hadn't bothered to call and tell her where I was in the first place. I spun back towards the door and stumbled as I passed the males still pulling sentry duty.

Dillon purred just off to my left. "She's night blind. Just look at her, all wide-eyed and wandering." His fingers tangled in my hair. "The truest earmark of royalty."

"Let her go," Mason commanded from somewhere to my right. A large hand closed over my arm and tugged me away, yanking hair from my head in the process. I found myself plastered against a body I assumed was Mason's by his sheer bulk. His grip tightened possessively.

"Mason." I slowly pulled back while trying to touch as little of him as possible. "Can I go now? Please?" He didn't answer.

Heavy footsteps thumped dully behind me. Then I was knocked aside, stumbling into the gingerbread porch railing and grabbing it for balance. A thick pop of knuckle on bone sounded, someone grunted, and the boards beneath my feet shuddered. Then a colder, firmer grip held me. I breathed in mint and felt the presence of irritated male.

"I don't care where you go or how you get there," Dillon said. "But get there fast." He dragged me along by the viselike grip on my arm. I heard the front door open and switches flipping as he smoothed his hand along the wall. The porch flooded with light.

My eyes swallowed the glare, focusing on Mason's supine body sprawled across the porch where, presumably, Dillon had punched him and knocked him out cold.

"Mason is young, and he'd never forgive himself for hurting you. I don't have that problem." He dragged me to the edge of the lawn and shoved me out into the street. "Now go before I decide having you is worth having my ass handed to me. And I'm old enough to know it's not."

"Thank you." I tossed the words over my shoulder. I used the sparse overhead street lamps to help me sort out cars from hedges and buildings. After a nervous sprint across the pavement, the neon glow of the diner's sign gave me direction. I took a few more lurching steps and pushed through the door into the restaurant.

For a change, Emma had hostess duty. Her gaze raked me from head to toe before directing her sight out the window and across the street. The curl in her upper lip bared more teeth than would make most of her patrons comfortable. I stepped up to the tiny podium covered in laminated menus. "We need to talk."

She shuffled the already tidy cards. "Now isn't a good time."

"Make time."

"Like you made time to call me?" She circled around and poked my shoulder with her finger, rocking me back on my heels. "You ran someone over and didn't think to spare five minutes to call me and tell me you were okay?"

I grabbed her wrist, twisting her hand over and under, just like she'd taught me. Using her momentum, I brought her hand behind her back, pushing up to show her I meant business. There was only one way out of this hold and she'd have to break her arm to do it. I felt pretty confident she wouldn't want the kids at table three to see that. "I'm sorry I didn't call. It was stupid and thoughtless of me, but I'm here now and I want answers."

She jerked her shoulder, testing my grip. When she only managed to pop her arm, she sighed. "Let's do this in the office."

I guided her forward. Situated behind the bustling kitchen, her tiny office held little else besides a secondhand desk and a chair that had seen better days before the five years we'd owned it. Corralling us inside, I released her arm and twisted the lock behind me.

She took her seat, rolling her worn chair beneath her battered desk and propping her elbows on the scarred surface. "What do you want to know?"

"I want it all. Everything you know about Clayton and Harper."

Her cheeks paled. "You want the truth?"

"It would be a nice change of pace."

She leaned back in her chair. "I found out by accident, you have to believe that. Otherwise, Harper never would have told me. He never meant for either of us to know."

"Okay." I could extend that much faith.

"I saw Clayton for the first time when you were young, around eleven or twelve and taken with a fever. You were inconsolable wanting your demon, so I went to find Harper."

"I remember." The fever had almost succeeded in killing me where Archer had failed. "I was bed-bound for a week." I did the math in my head. "That means you were fifteen and he was sixteen."

She nodded absently. "I discovered Harper meeting with Clayton in the courtyard. I didn't recognize him, so I hid and eavesdropped on their conversation. They argued because Harper wanted to stay inside the Askaran royal house to gather intelligence for the Evanti resistance. Clayton tried to talk him out of it, saying there were enough informants already, but Harper wouldn't listen."

Dull, throbbing pain filled my head. I rubbed my temples in deep circles but got no relief. "You're telling me Harper was a spy for the freeborn legion?"

It made a perfect kind of sense. I'd had the puzzle pieces,

but they never clicked into place. That explained his flippant remark that he'd only stayed in Askara for me. He'd had a choice, a life, and a family outside of what we'd shared, but I hadn't realized it until he'd brought me to this realm.

I hadn't thought about the hows or whys of Harper's relationship with the colony since I'd lost him. If someone talked about him, I walked away. If they asked about him, I didn't answer. I had been so intent, so focused on surviving, I hadn't looked beyond the end of my own nose.

Emma had been right. Denial was a river and I had been drowning in it.

"Yes, he was."

"And you never told me?" I kicked her desk as hurt and anger mingled into a volatile cocktail within me. She frowned, so I kicked it again. "I could have helped. I could have done something to make a difference."

"No, you couldn't have. Harper risked enough for us all." What little color she'd had left faded. "If you had been caught aiding the cause, then your punishment would have fallen to me, Maddie. *Me.* Not them. I couldn't keep hurting you. Something in me died more every time I broke you. Harper knew that, and he wanted to spare us both."

I let the horror of the past wash over me. Trying to stop the memories never worked, it only made the next time that much worse. I centered my attention on the present, on this conversation, and the answers I had to have.

"Did Harper love me at all? Was that part truth?" I had to know. "Or did he just use me to get information on my family?"

Emma's face tightened as she tried for a smile that fell short of the mark. "He loved you very much. You have to remember he was raised alongside us before he even knew about his father or Clayton." Her voice quieted. "You thought his wings made him an angel, but he wasn't, not even close. You were a sister to him. He would have given his life for you, but even if things hadn't deteriorated, he still couldn't have taken you to mate and wouldn't have taken you as a lover."

There had been a time not long ago when I would have argued the point with her. I had planned a life with Harper and I thought he'd wanted the same with me.

It hadn't been until meeting Clayton that I realized what that relationship would have lacked. Heat, desire and passion— all things Clayton brought out in me. Things I hadn't been aware of to notice their absence between Harper and me.

I might be able to agree with Emma now, but I needed to hear her explanation since I would never know his. "But all this time you let me believe he and I would have been together here, in this new realm."

Her mouth opened and then closed on what she would have said. "We would have told you. After lying for so long, there wasn't an easy way out. Then he didn't come home and I didn't know what to do." She stared into her hands as if they held the answers. "He was gone. And we were alone." She wiped her down-turned cheek. When she looked up, her face was dry, but no less mottled.

I wanted to forgive her. I knew she had suffered, but so had I. "Do you know how much it would have meant to me these past few years? To know Harper had kin?"

Her runes snapped into evidence, pale purple and darkening. "Don't play the martyr. Not with me. You would have fallen into Clayton's arms and you know it. I couldn't let you do that to yourself." She pushed back in her chair. "Even Clayton deserved better. He deserved knowing you saw him and not a replacement for his brother." Just as quickly, her own unique glamour covered the evidence of her emotions. "When I saw you two together that first night, I knew we had all made mistakes too big to take back."

Her fingers crept across the desktop, reaching for mine. I stood and paced. Two steps forward, two steps back. I needed more room, more air.

I struggled to hold on to my waning rage. I couldn't blame her for loving me more than anyone else ever had. My weakness had forced her into the role of protector, and she took it seriously. But I needed all the cards on the table before I could put this behind us.

"What about Clayton?" I eyed her sheepish expression. "You wanted me to think the worst of him. Why?"

Her open palms slammed against the desktop. "That arrogant bastard could have saved you. He could have made Harper stop playing hero. He could have taken you away and given you a better life somewhere far away from Askara and Archer, but he didn't. He wouldn't save you." Another tear tracked down her cheek. "I begged him, but he refused to endanger the lives of his precious colonists."

Everything was always so clear cut to Emma. She felt emotion so deeply, so absolutely, nothing else mattered when those she loved were hurting.

"Clayton was right to leave me, to leave us as we were. Harper gave his life to help his people earn the beginnings of freedom. I know it hurts, but you can't cheapen his sacrifice by making his actions sound impetuous." I sighed, facing another harsh truth. "You and I would have endured as well, as countless generations of Askaran females had before us. There was nothing so special about us that we should have been saved—except for the worth Harper placed on us." I looked at her. "He was so much more than I ever realized."

I'd had another revelation as well. "That's why you hate

Clayton so much," I surmised, feeling the rest of my anger fall away. "He knew firsthand the risks Harper and others legionaries had undertaken. Because of that, he understood the life of one princess wasn't worth the risk to hundreds of freed Evanti and their families."

Emma offered six words in her defense. "You were worth it to me."

Of course her reason would have been me. She never thought of herself. I didn't think she knew how. I sat on the edge of her desk and reached out to her.

"You did what you thought was right. We all did." I took her damp hand in mine. "And I couldn't have asked for a better big sister."

I squeezed her fingers. She squeezed back. Forgiven and forgotten.

Her brow creased. "What will you do now? I mean, about this thing between you and Clayton?"

"I don't know. I care about him, a lot, but so much has happened so fast. I don't know where my head is." Or my heart, but neither of us were ready to hear that said aloud.

"He won't pressure you to decide." This time her voice held grudging respect.

I laughed, breaking the tension just enough for us both to smile and really mean it. "I know. He said he doesn't want to see me until I'm..." My cheeks heated. "Well, not for two more days."

"I think you're making the right choice. Both of you have a lot to think about."

Behind me, the doorknob rattled. A few sharp raps of knuckle on hollow core door ended our impromptu meeting. I turned the deadbolt and found Marci poised with her fist raised to knock again.

"What do you need?" I wedged a stopper beneath the open door.

Her gaze darted across the hall towards the kitchen. She didn't get a chance to speak before the scent of char filled the small office. I coughed and fanned my face. "What is that smell?"

"I had just finished my rounds up front when a customer commented on the stink. A couple even left before I could find the problem." She pointed to her nose. "I would have said something sooner, but my allergies are acting up and I can't smell a damn thing."

"Lynn." Emma shoved us aside, mumbling. "What is that girl up to now? Can't turn my back for a minute..."

I followed Emma's bouncing gait into the kitchen. Rounding the corner, we walked into a disaster. Lynn hunched over the telephone, curling the cord around her finger while ignoring the Dutch oven left bubbling too high on the stovetop. My eyes watered even from the doorway.

A resigned sigh shifted Emma from unburdened sister back into business owner. "Lynn." The woman spun around and hung up guiltily. "You know we have a policy against making personal phone calls while on the clock."

Lynn pointed to the phone. "Sorry, but that was Andrew. He called to tell me Clayton organized a last-minute raid. They've just left for Askara."

I blurted out the first thing that came to mind. "He's not well enough to travel."

Lynn's stare said she felt differently. "Andrew said it was sudden. Clayton got a tip about a pocket of slaves being held under light guard in the outlands." She sighed, clearly unhappy to be without her male. Somehow that managed to earn points with me regardless. "He said to expect him home in two days. Three days tops."

Emma turned down the soup and gave it a quick stir. "Thanks for the update, but that's no excuse to neglect your duties. If you can't get your act together, then I'll have to let you go. This place pays all of our bills. If you burn it to the ground while making goo-goo voices to your male over the phone, then we'll all be ruined." She lifted the spoon to taste the stew, winced, then lifted it off the stove and poured it down the drain. Hours of work, wasted.

Lynn answered quickly, rushing to grab a rag and wipe the broth drying on the stovetop. "I'm sorry. I'll try harder, I promise. I'm just not myself when Andrew has to leave."

"I can sympathize." Emma filled the blackened pot with soapy water while eyeing her now-wary employee. "But Marci's male is in rotation too. She works part time and has two little ones underfoot as well. I don't see her setting my kitchen on fire while cooing goodbyes to Lester."

Lynn stared at the chipped tile floor. "I'll start the dishes."

"No," Emma said. "I'll take the dishes. You finish up with the customers we have left. Go ahead and flip the sign while you're up there. No one else will want to smell this while they're eating anyway."

I watched Lynn's slumped retreat but couldn't muster up the energy to feel sorry for her. "What about me?"

She pointed to the chair where Clayton had sat the night before. I ran my fingers across the chrome trim and faux leather piping. The seat was gutted with cotton batting fluffing out of the seams. We'd duct taped it once before relegating the chair to the kitchen where it would spend the remainder of its days as a stepping stool.

"Are you going to sit down or pet it?" Emma asked.

I stepped away from the chair and the memory of its last occupant. "I don't feel like sitting down. How about I finish up the dishes and you handle the close-out paperwork? Crunching those little numbers gives me a migraine."

Elbow deep in suds, she shrugged. "Yeah, I can handle that. You always forget to carry the one anyway."

I tossed her a tattered rag from the pile, which she used to dry herself on her way past. Alone in the kitchen, it was hard not to think about Clayton. How he'd soaked his shirt and then mine. Or how I'd slipped and he carried me from the kitchen. And those kisses...

"Hey." Emma's head poked around the corner. "Did you see where I put that bag of receipts?"

I glanced over and had to blink a few times before I saw her clearly. "Which ones did you lose this time, the dailies or weeklies?" I asked, wiping my cheek against my forearm.

She looked at me and laughed softly. "I guess it was already too late for warnings." She crossed the room to wrap me in exactly the kind of hug I needed. "You love him, don't you?"

"I don't know," I answered her honestly. "I just...hurt. I saw him a few hours ago, and I know he's okay, or at least he will be, but I miss him. I didn't want to leave him, and now that he's gone..." I paused, "...I'm afraid. What if he doesn't come back? What if he's wrong? What if the only thing between us is heat and pheromones?"

She pulled back to look me in the eye. "You can what-if yourself to death, but that boy has loved you for half of your life already. I used to worry what would happen if Harper's feelings for you ever did change. Clayton would have let you have his brother." Her fingers tightened on me. "That's how you should measure his devotion. Not by what he wants *from* you, though make no mistake—he wants it all, but what he wants *for* you.

There's nothing within his power he wouldn't do to make you happy. That includes giving you up." She scrunched up her nose. "Now I've invested far too many years hating his guts to go all soft on him now. Don't think just because I'm being all nice and sisterly to you that I'll cut him any slack." She winked and went back to search for her missing papers.

I sank my hands in the warm, foamy water and scrubbed, allowing my head time to catch up to my heart.

Chapter Thirteen

Three days later, the diner buzzed with typical Sunday morning conversation, each layered voice droning until only the collective hum remained.

"Here you go, Mr. Lawrence." I unloaded my tray. "Grilled cheese sandwich on wheat with tomato soup."

"Thank you, Madelyn." His eyes squinted behind Coke-bottle lenses. "You look lovely as always."

"Why thank you very much."

His spoon shook in my direction. "You could stand to put on a little weight, though. Elsa always had such a nice, round figure." He scratched his chin. "They just don't make women like her anymore."

I offered him condolence. "You were a lucky man to have had her all those years."

His head wobbled in a shaky bob. "Yes, I believe I was." He filled his spoon, and I tucked my tray against my chest, leaving him to enjoy his meal.

Past the crowded tables, I headed for the kitchen with a pocketful of fresh orders for the cook. The back of a head full of blonde curls came into view as I stepped into the galley-style kitchen. Emma glanced over her shoulder and grinned.

"Business is booming today." She tapped her wooden spoon

in time with her words. "I can almost see my new Viking range. Only seven hundred dollars left to go and it's industrial stove, here I come."

"If we have a few more days like today, we'll have that sucker paid for, crated and headed this way." I passed over the tickets covered in my very best waitress scrawl, meaning only Emma could decipher them.

The small bell hung over the diner door tinkled. I glanced towards the hall and smoothed my hands down my shirt and apron.

"Expecting someone?"

"No." Clayton had only come to the diner once in the last five years. So, yeah, I was crazy because my pulse kicked up and my palms got sweaty just thinking about him walking through that door.

Then the bell tinkled three more times in rapid succession. This time Emma's face lit up. She had a standing date every Sunday with three gentlemen and it sounded as if they had arrived.

She killed the flame on the stove and shifted the large pot off the burner, then cleaned her hands on the towel hanging from her apron. I pulled my pad and pen out and followed her up front, right into an ambush.

"Emma! Emma! Emma!" Eager cherub-faced triplets tugged at her pants and apron.

"Well, if it isn't the three most handsome men alive." She fanned her face with her hand. After tweaking each button nose, she gathered them in for a tight hug, which they allowed with typical male reluctance. "It's been too long, guys. Who said you could grow up on me?"

"Emma," Jared sighed. "We saw you..." He turned to his brother Ben for confirmation. Ben shrugged, turning to Parker instead.

"Last Wednesday!" Parker squealed.

She slapped her forehead with the heel of her palm. "Of course. What was I thinking? How's that leg doing today, Parker?"

"Em-ma." Parker groaned. "You sound just like Momma."

"Sorry," she said. "I forget how grown you are sometimes." Then she looked up to their mother. "Hello, Dana."

"Good afternoon. Madelyn, we'll take our usual, please."

Emma ruffled the hair of the nearest boy. "Follow Miss Maddie, guys, she'll take good care of you while I go get your order ready."

I led the trio plus mom to a booth in the rear of the restaurant and watched the boys pile in one on top of the other, elbowing for room as they leaned across the tabletop. Dana slipped onto the bench seat opposite them.

With their drink orders filled, I returned to the table. "I'll be right back with some crayons and coloring books." The boy's hands slapped the table, eagerly staking claim to their section of workspace.

At the podium, I bent down and separated three thin booklets and three packets of crayons from the second-shelf basket. The last box's bottom fell open, spilling the colors across the floor just as the tiny bell tinkled again.

"I'll be right with you." I gathered the rolling crayons.

"There's no hurry."

Fear straightened my spine, jerking me upright. I hit my head on the podium's overhang, but ignored the dull ache and reached into the topmost bin filled with wrapped silverware. I fumbled a dull knife free of its napkin wrapper and faced my customer.

"Jacob, I'm sure you'll understand when I say you aren't welcome here anymore."

He stepped forward and my hand tightened on the knife. Blunt it might be, but enough force would slow him down until Emma could arrive.

He took a half step back when he noticed my hands remained concealed. "I had to see you and I thought it would be safe now that, well, it's been five days." He coughed through his embarrassment. "I wanted to apologize. I have a problem with caffeine, I do, but I swear I've been doing better about drinking decaf. It's just that times have been bad for me. I never meant for things to get so far out of hand that day." The black-and-white tile floor held his attention. "I have issues with your family, but all of us do. With you being like you were, and the coffee, I just lost it." He glanced up. "I had to say I'm sorry. That wasn't me, and if you ever need to go to Harper's grave, just call ahead and I'll make myself scarce." He turned to leave. "I don't expect forgiveness, but I owed you some explanation."

"Wait." I half expected Emma to barrel out at any moment to separate his head from his neck. "I appreciate you coming to tell me, but you have to get help before something like this happens again. The next female might not be so lucky."

I couldn't say I forgave him. I didn't, maybe never could. I couldn't say it was okay, because it wasn't. No matter the extenuating circumstances, he had problems, and I wasn't looking to solve them.

He ducked his head, pushing back through the door and outside where I watched until he disappeared from sight. My hold on the knife eased. Then, on second thought, I slipped it into my apron pocket. Just in case.

I gathered the loose crayons and coloring books, carrying them back to the kids. Dana sat with her hands folded and stared at me, smiling just enough to make me nervous. "Sorry for the delay. I'll go check on your order."

Ducking into the kitchen, I ladled three mugs of tomato soup and grabbed wedges of grilled cheese sandwiches from a blissfully unaware Emma, then carried it all on a tray to the waiting boys.

My fingers looped through the mug handles and settled the smaller portions of soup onto the red and white checkerboard tablecloth. Choruses of "thank you" from Emma's favorite patrons made me grin as I fished a handful of saltine packets from my apron, dropping them with a few extra napkins onto the table. "Will there be anything else, sirs?"

Three sets of baby blues glanced up, grinning as they elbowed and shoved to hoard the most crackers from one another. "No, ma'am," they chimed in triplicate.

"Dana, are you sure I can't get you something?"

"No, I'm just fine, thank you. I ate an early lunch with Clayton and the new arrivals."

I exhaled slowly, counting backwards from ten and telling myself it didn't chafe to know she'd seen him today and I hadn't. "Great. I hope they're settling in okay. I know the acclimation process can come as a shock."

"Yes, today was full of surprises."

I waited for an explanation, but she didn't offer one.

"Well, enjoy your meal and I'll check back in with you in a few." I escaped to the short hall separating the kitchen from Emma's office, needing a minute to myself. Between Dana's annoying cryptic remarks and Jacob's confession, I had a lot to digest and I didn't think the Rolaids I kept for customers in my apron pocket were going to be any help.

The worn paneling gave beneath my back. I heard a sharp

click and the murmur of voices seconds before the emergency-exit door popped open. The alarm didn't sound, which was going to get Emma in serious trouble with the health inspector one day.

I squinted against the glaring light pouring in from outside. Lynn's shoulder bumped my own, jostling me aside in her haste. Marci followed on her heels and touched a gentle hand to my arm as she passed. They both entered the kitchen with hurried steps. Neither said a word. How strange.

The door swung wide again and Clayton stepped through it. My chest tightened, wound by the convergence of relief to see him home safe and the knowledge he had come for me. I'd done a lot of thinking the last three days and had made my decision. I just didn't know how to go about telling him what I needed him to hear.

"I need to talk to you." He reached for my hand. "I've brought someone you'll want to see."

"I can't just leave." I laughed. "Emma—"

"Has Lynn and Marci to cover for you. You need to come outside with me."

He compressed the metal bar with his hip. Pulling me along with him, we stepped into the narrow alley running behind the store meant for deliveries and trash collections. I didn't see anything, or more to the point, anyone.

"There's no easy way to tell you this."

My palms dampened. Who could he have brought? What if this was a trick to lure me away from the bustling flow of the diner's steady lunch traffic? He was the colony leader. Maybe he couldn't risk the social entanglement with a half Askaran.

If I made a scene, he wouldn't want witnesses. Would he tell me our relationship was over before it began? I tried to steady my hands shaking lightly within his. Did he know how scared I was to lose him? How the thought terrified me until I'd tossed and turned each night he'd been away?

"After you left me at the inn, I received word from a legion contact posted in Askara. He'd heard from a slave in your mother's service at First Court."

I exhaled in a sharp rush that huffed between us. Not personal. Business. That I could handle.

His warm thumbs rubbed over my skin. "The slave reported that your mother had kept a golden cage in her private chamber for a number of years. It was always empty while he attended her, but curiosity got the better of him once and he stepped inside the cage to look around. Lines were scored into the bottom, like someone had been marking time." Clayton glanced up, finally meeting my eyes. "Someone was being kept there."

"That's hardly unusual." I hated remembering the culture I'd been born into, where cruelty was applauded and abuse commonplace. "A lot of the nobility have eccentric tastes."

His slow motions ceased. "Yes, but he had reason to believe that I would want to know of this slave in particular."

My mind struggled with the implications. Only one male would have drawn his personal interest. "Harper?" I forced the name past my suddenly dry lips as I waited for Clayton's confirmation. No wonder he had left so quickly. Even wounded, the remote possibility of reuniting with his brother must have spurred him into action. "You think he's alive?"

Clayton reached into his pocket and pulled out the braided leather bracelet Harper had been wearing the last time I'd seen him. The night he didn't came home. I took the slight weight into my hand, turning it over and smoothing my thumb across our names. "Where did you get this?"

"Our informant found it hidden in the bottom of the cage. He recognized the names and went to find a legion contact he trusted."

"We have to go to him." My fist closed around the bracelet.

"No, we don't." Clayton palmed my shoulders. Gravel crunched beneath my shoes as he twisted me around to face the open alley. I leaned into his strength as my eyes caught on Mason escorting my guest. "It's all right." His fingers skated over my skin, soothing me with his warmth. "Just remember to breathe."

Mason's approach was hindered by the support he offered the second male's slight frame. He stood with his eyes downcast, staring in the vicinity of my feet. His blond hair hung loose around his face with circles darkening his eyes. His skin looked gaunt and discolored, none of which I should have been able to see. His fading glamour flickered.

"I don't understand."

A graveled voice issued from the weakened male. "He's brought you a gift, Maddie." When he looked up, his full black eyes sparked instant recognition. "Unless you would have him return me?"

Hearing my name on his lips, my mouth fell open. "Harper?" I loosened my hold on Clayton. "Is that really you?" I stepped forward, hopeful, but unwilling to believe, so afraid this would be a trick of my mind and not reality.

"Who else would it be?" He shook off Mason's hold and opened his arms to me.

I ran into them without hesitation. My hands slipped around his waist, so much thinner than I remembered. I felt his spine where my fingers met at the small of his back as bone almost punched through delicate skin and the thin flannel shirt hanging from his lean frame.

Spiced incense tickled my nose. His fragile heart beat softly beneath my ear. "I thought I'd lost you." Hot tears spilled over my cheeks to soak his shirt with my happiness.

Harper buried his fingers in my hair and tucked me close. "I thought I was lost too."

I took his beloved face between my palms. My thumbs dipped into the hollow planes of his cheeks. "Have you been in Askara this whole time? How did you escape?"

"The night I left you and Emma, I found Marcus and Clayton too late. Their intelligence was wrong about the location. Because of your ascendancy, there was twice the number of guards they had been told to expect. They were ambushed just outside of this realm." A steadying breath rattled through his chest. "I helped Father carry the wounded legionaries to safety while Clayton covered our backs. When we circled around to search for survivors, an arrow sliced through Father's wing."

Harper's eyes closed. "The archers took advantage of his freefall. By the time I reached him, there were dozens of shafts piercing his body, too many to safely remove. Clayton was wounded while trying to reach us. The fall knocked him unconscious, so I had the remaining legionaries carry him home while I stayed with Father. He died in my arms. And I was captured."

"If not for me—"

"Then positive change wouldn't have been set into motion." His glamour flickered again, revealing an almost skeletal frame shrouded in tight, black skin. "After I took you away, Nesvia blamed your disappearance on your mother. She has planned a coup to overthrow the throne of Askara. It's taken many years to gather the proper support, but now she has it, and won't rest until she's taken the crown." His coarse voice held hope. "She plans to abolish slavery. It will be a long path to our people's freedom, but your sister has taken the first step."

"I don't know what to say. I didn't know her well, but I always thought she was grounded by Rideal." I grinned. "Mother must be livid."

"I wouldn't know. She vanished two months past with her private guard and half her servants. I've been a guest of the outlands since then." His eyes lit with sincerity. "I mentioned to Clayton that in a few months' time, once things have settled, you might want to contact Nesvia. You could help negotiate for our side. You're half and half, the perfect mediator for our cause."

I pulled his face down to mine and pressed a kiss to his cheek. "I would gladly help the others bargain for their freedom."

A growl rose up behind me. I glanced over my shoulder to Clayton, and the sound rumbled into silence.

"I don't think my brother likes you so close to me." Harper cracked a smile. "But then, he never did."

"Madelyn is free to make her own choices."

Harper chuckled softly. "I had hoped in five years things would have progressed. Are you still playing knight errant? Still coveting her from the shadows?"

"What would you have me do?" Something bordering perilously close to despair weighted his words. "You left her grieving, as your widow."

"It was hardly my intention, brother. I never planned for any of this to happen. I didn't plan for Father to die, or to abandon Maddie and Emma. Certainly you can't imagine I planned to sit in a gilded cage as a pet for the queen?"

Clayton turned his back to us. "I don't blame you for Father's death. I don't blame you for any of this." His fingers linked behind his head as he continued to stare off into the distance.

I pulled from Harper's arms and waited until Mason helped him regain his balance. Then I walked until the toes of my shoes touched Clayton's. He looked down at me. My neck dipped back and our gazes collided. "I have something to tell you."

His grim expression turned graver. "I'll hear anything you have to say."

His gaze roved over my face as if memorizing it. He stood board straight. Tall, proud and hurting behind the illusion he projected. I could feel it. I knew he would offer his brother to me, even though he knew it had never been what Harper wanted. I just don't think he realized I knew that now too.

All Clayton needed were the words. A command he could follow like the good little legionnaire he'd been raised.

My arms linked around his neck as I tunneled my fingers in his dark curls and drew his reluctant mouth down to mine.

His lips were tight and unmoving, so I softened mine to press light kisses across the hard seam of his mouth. I flicked my tongue out to taste him, drawing in a hint of citrus. He groaned a rumbling sound that moved through me, tightening my stomach with anticipation. I nipped at him, forcing his lips harder to mine.

"Please, don't tempt me."

"I don't mean to. I want you to know I've made my choice." My throat tightened and tears choked my words. "I am so grateful that Harper is alive, and I need him to be a part of my life."

"I meant what I said. You are free to make your own choices. I wouldn't have you claim either of us unless it was what you wanted."

"I know what I want." I focused on keeping the tremor from my voice. "And even if Harper wanted me, and we both know he

197

doesn't, I wouldn't choose any differently. I've had days to think about everything you and Emma have told me." I swallowed past the fear that something for him might have changed. "I was miserable without you. I couldn't breathe for fear you wouldn't come back to me, and finding Harper doesn't change anything between us."

Clayton's eyes darkened, dilated, and drew me into them. "I want to believe that." He walked me backwards until my shoulders hit the brick wall of the diner. His fingers dug into my hips, aligning me with the part of him I'd been curious about since our fall from Emasen. "But I have to know it's me you want."

I pulled my hands from around his neck and smoothed them down his chest until they reached the waist of his pants. Hooking my fingers through the tiny belt loops, I pulled him closer, until I felt how hard, how ready he was to have me.

He lowered his face to the curve of my neck and thrust once against me, groaning just below my ear.

"Your brother is watching."

"Let him watch."

"You know, for such a straight-laced male, I'm beginning to think you're a closet exhibitionist."

The crack of metal on brick echoed through the alley. I jerked my gaze from Clayton and found my sister standing in the doorway with her hands on her hips. "Lynn said Clayton had a message for you." Her eyes zeroed in on where my fingers looped through his jeans and dipped into his pockets. "Silly me for not realizing he would hide it in his pants."

Silence settled around us. Things I should have said scrolled rapidly through my mind, but Harper's voice cut through the tension thickening the air.

"All this time and you two still haven't learned to play

nice?"

Emma stiffened. Her spine snapped ramrod straight and her eyes rounded. The meat of her palm slapped the wall. Braced against the bricks, she faced him. "I thought you were dead."

"I hear that a lot." The corner of his mouth twitched. "But, as you can see, I am very much alive."

"You don't understand..." Mortar crumbled beneath her fingers. "We had a funeral. And you have a grave. There's a blank marker because Maddie couldn't let you go. I didn't want to let you go either, but one of us had to be strong or we wouldn't have survived." She glanced at the gouged brick and sealant then dropped her arm. "I couldn't think about you being alive. I just couldn't—"

His unsteady steps closed the distance between them. Narrow arms banded around her, pulling her to rest against him. "Shh." His lips brushed the corner of hers. "You don't have to be strong anymore." He pressed another kiss to her forehead. "Everything is going to be all right."

He nuzzled aside her hair, brushing their cheeks together. Silver engulfed the black of his eyes. His lips brushed her jaw and traveled upward towards the shell of her ear where he whispered as he had our last night in Rihos. Whatever he said brought the crown of her head up fast enough to catch his jaw. He winced and Emma jerked from his arms.

Coordination failed her as she scuttled backwards until her frantically seeking hands closed over the metal exit door. I glanced between Harper and Emma. She looked nervous while he appeared resolved. What could he have said to spook her?

"I'm glad you're here—safe. I meant I'm glad you're safe." She turned wide, glazed eyes on me. "I need to get back to work. Lynn is alone in my kitchen. She could burn the place down while my back is turned."

Harper stalked slowly closer, his every forward step made her gasp and the door moan where her halfling strength dented the metal in her hand.

This leaner, darker Harper didn't seem to care. I saw my sister reflected in the mirrored shine of his predatory gaze and felt the ground beneath me shift yet again. I recognized his expression as one worn on Clayton's face whenever he looked at me.

Her voice came out as little more than a whisper. "I think you should go."

"She's right." I stepped to her side and addressed the steadily advancing male. "You should rest. We have to get back to work anyway." And I needed to speak with my sister—alone.

He stared past me to Emma. "When does your shift end?"

"It varies."

"Your shift." He stopped. "When does it end?"

She didn't answer. Their silent standoff lasted until Clayton cleared his throat.

"I should go. The others are waiting for me at the inn." He raised his voice just enough to carry. "And my brother needs to rest whether he wants to admit it or not."

"Come on." I pried Emma's fingers from crimped steel. "We still have four hours left on the clock."

Harper's eyes glinted. I realized I'd just given him what he wanted without meaning to.

"What are you up to?" I had a feeling that sparkle in his eyes meant trouble for Emma.

The lopsided grin I loved so well lifted his lips. "I can't hold down solid food. I had hoped to persuade Emma to bring me some tomato basil soup after work. It's still her specialty, isn't it?" His gaze slid back to Emma. "After all the years spent perfecting a food for her picky little sister to eat, it should be."

Emma ducked into the hall. "It is. Wait here and I'll pour you a to-go portion."

He frowned apologetically. "My body is still on Askaran time. I don't think I can manage yet, but if you wait four hours then your timing would be perfect." His teeth flashed in a quick smile. "Of course, that's only if you don't mind. I wouldn't want to inconvenience you."

Emma's face pinked. Her lavender scrollwork glowed against the blush building in her cheeks. She cleared her throat and kept her gaze pointedly away from the male in front of her. "Fine. I'll bring you soup after closing."

"Thank you."

I would have called him on his antics, but Clayton's warm hand caressed my side and Harper's machinations ceased to matter. "When can I see you again?"

"Didn't you hear?" I smiled. "I get off work in four hours." I let my voice trail off. "If you're interested."

"I am most definitely interested." His smile was wicked. "Figment and I have plans tonight. If you aren't busy, maybe you would like to join us?"

I rose up on tiptoe and pressed a kiss to his lips, sealing our deal. "It's a date."

Emma's iron grip closed over my upper arm. "Back to work, remember?"

I almost growled, or maybe Clayton had. Either way, a soft hum of disappointment moved through my lips.

"See you in four." He moved into place to support Harper for the walk back to the inn. Mason followed them down the alley, around the corner and out of sight.

I followed Emma into the hall. When the door closed behind us, I dug in my heels. She would either stop walking or have to drag me.

She jerked my arm. "Come on, I need to get back to my kitchen."

"No," I said, standing my ground. "You need to tell me what happened out there." A shudder moved through my arm where she held it.

"He's alive." Emma glanced at me and light caught the shine of tears held in her eyes. "You saw him. He's really here."

"Yes I did, and he is." I covered her hand with mine and found it cold. "You didn't imagine it. He's really come home."

She nodded once before her back hit the oak paneling. Fabric rasped as she slid to the floor. Her head braced on her arms, her arms across her kneecaps. Her shoulders shook so hard she appeared to rock in place.

I sank to my knees beside her. "Are you all right?" I heard her lungs fill with air and force out a hushed sob. I touched her shoulder. "Emma?"

When I pried her face from her arms, blood smeared her bottom lip where she'd bitten it trying to hold back her cries. I rushed to the kitchen and grabbed a towel, pausing long enough to dampen it.

Falling into a crouch at her side, I wiped her eyes and mouth. How many nights had she done this? Hurt this way and never said a word?

"You should have told me." I sat beside her, brushing her hair from her face.

Emma snorted. "Why? You thought you were in love with Harper. I couldn't tell you I loved him too. You would have hated me for it."

I sank to the floor beside her until our hips met. Then I reached over and broke the tense line of her body by pulling her head down to rest on my shoulder as I wrapped my arms around her. "You're right," I agreed with reluctance. "I was too wrapped up in my own pain to notice you were hurting." I kissed the top of her head. "You've always been so strong."

Her breath warmed my neck. "Maddie, I don't want to be strong anymore. I'm so tired."

I hugged her even closer. "You don't have to be. I'm fine, thanks to you. It's time for you to focus on what you want." I paused. "What will make you happy?"

"I don't know. I haven't really thought about it."

"What about Harper?" She shivered at the mention of his name. I had to ask, "What did he say to you out there?"

Her fingers linked and tightened until her knuckles shone white. "He said he'd waited long enough." She swallowed. "He means to claim me."

"Isn't that a good thing?"

Her head shook. "I thought he was dead. I dated men and..." her voice quieted, "...I did things." Warm moisture saturated my shirt and the skin beneath her cheek. "Things he'll hate me for."

I grabbed her chin between my fingers, forcing her to look up at me. "You can't believe that."

"I shouldn't have given up so easily. I should have been more like you. If I'd just held on longer—"

"Stop it." I grabbed her shoulders and shook. "If you'd been like me, neither of us would have survived. You're the one who ran the diner, paid our bills and kept a roof over our heads. You saved us every bit as much as Harper did. He'll know that. He won't hold your time apart against you."

She continued to stare at the floor.

"If you want, I can take the soup to Harper when I meet up with Clayton." I smiled while she couldn't see it. "Dana's there. I'm sure she won't mind helping out an old acquaintance."

Emma's head snapped up. Her tattoos glowed violet against her red face. "You're not funny." Her lips tipped up at the corner.

I gave her a shove. "Come on. You don't have to decide anything today." I stood and reached down to help her up. "He's safe. That's what matters. The rest will fall into place."

She shoved me back. "You're right." She wiped her face with her palms and willed her glamour into place. "It's not like he can make me do something I don't want to, right?"

I coughed into my hand. If Harper had set out to claim her, I doubted anything would stop him. The male was nothing if not determined. "Right."

Chapter Fourteen

Emma refused to take the stairs, so I left her standing in the damp grass with her feet shoulder's width apart. Her hands clasped over Tupperware marked with her name in bold letters as if daring Harper not to return it. Her lips were set in a stubborn line, her gaze sharpened to a glare directed at a second-story window. I didn't know if she wanted to get in some practice or if she'd actually seen someone up there.

The hardwood panel thumped beneath my knuckles. Seconds later, Dana opened the door. Her gaze slid over me to Emma.

"Harper mentioned you were coming. Is that his soup? He asked if you could bring it up to his room when you arrived." Dana pushed the door open while continuing to pretend I didn't exist, which suited me just fine. Her panties were in a perpetual state of twist and I wasn't about to offer any assistance.

Emma fingered the container with a frown, sealing and unsealing the lid until she caught herself and forced the top back into place. "Does he think I'm going to spoonfeed him too?" She took grudging steps forward and indicated I should enter before she followed me into the lobby.

Dana shut the door with a soft click. "Madelyn, I'm sorry, but whatever you came for will have to wait. Emma will be upstairs with Harper and I'm right in the middle of something."

"I'm sorry too, but Clayton asked me to meet him here."

She paused. Fresh from work, I smelled of French fries and wore red soup stains on my T-shirt and jeans. She smelled of something flowery and wore black slacks with a trim blue top that accentuated a figure you'd never guess had produced three little boys all at once.

"All right." She stepped aside. "You can wait for him here in the lobby if you'd like."

The trio of boys in question tore through the room almost on cue. Parker's cast kicked over a box filled with packing peanuts and newspaper. They all skidded to a stop and looked up sheepishly. "Sorry, Mom," they said as each boy scooped Styrofoam bits to his chest.

Then they saw Emma. "What are you doing here?" Ben eagerly tugged at her rolled-up sleeve.

"I came to drop off some soup for Harper. What are you guys up to?"

"Mason's taking us to a ballgame." His voice rose with excitement. "All the males are playing out in the field behind our school. Only he can't because he promised to take us. He said if we behaved he'd even buy us nachos."

Dana shook her head in a resigned kind of way. "Boys will be boys," she said under her breath.

"That's great, guys." Emma looked past them to the narrow staircase leading to the second-floor bedrooms. She jerked her attention back to the children. "Remember your manners and be nice to Mr. Mason."

"We will."

Each boy took a turn embracing Emma. Then they each stood their ground for the barest fraction of a minute it took their mother to buss their cheeks. I rated a trio of careless waves thrown over their retreating shoulders.

While Dana ushered the boys outside to their chaperone, and Emma picked at her Tupperware lid, the wrongness of the room caught my attention. Boxes were stacked everywhere. Blank spaces on the walls called my attention to where portraits had once hung. Family portraits as I recalled.

Curtains were pulled down or aside, opening the room to the outside. She could be planning to remodel. I peered into the nearest box, then straightened, catching myself and moving away from temptation. "What's with the boxes?"

Dana went to the nearest box. She began wrapping ceramic figurines in newspaper and sorting them. "The boys and I are leaving town."

I stopped in my tracks and spun to face her, trying to keep my jaw off the floor. "Where will you go? Why will you go?"

"The news of your sister's attempted rise to power means more rescues can be made undetected." She shrugged. "This town is getting crowded. I don't think when Marcus started the colony he ever imagined his sons would be so successful in filling it." She smoothed a hand across the check-in desk counter. "I've registered hundreds of Evanti and their wives, but now it's time to move on. Start a new colony, a new life for me and the boys."

"Is it safe?" On second thought, the question was a dumb one. Clayton would never allow anyone to be harmed on his watch.

She folded a blanket and settled it inside an opened box. "Clayton would never send anyone out alone without protection. He assigned Dillon and a few other males to go ahead and secure the property and supplies we'll need to begin. We should be gone within the week, taking three of the larger families and a half dozen of the unmated males."

Emma didn't seem surprised. I'd been the only one left out of the loop. For once, it bothered me. I'd been awakened. I wanted a stake in the lives of those around me as well as my own. Resolve coursed through me. No more standing on the fringe. Starting with Dana could only make interaction with everyone else that much easier.

"Is this because of me and Clayton?"

She crinkled a ball of paper. "Yes and no." Rounding the desk, she dropped onto the floral-print sofa and patted the plump cushion beside her. "I haven't been very kind to you. Not really."

I took the seat she offered and, reaching down deep, I tried. Forgetting our last encounter would be impossible. The words she'd spoken in anger and the almost tangible need I'd had to break her as I'd once been broken were open sores left to fester between us. I pushed that aside for later contemplation and drew on the core of common decency Emma had instilled in me.

"I haven't exactly been charitable to you, either."

The earth didn't stop spinning. The sky didn't fall. I perked up. This coexisting thing might be doable.

"Can I ask you something?" Dana's blue eyes met mine.

"I guess."

"Are you serious about Clayton?"

I shifted on the sofa, wanting to blame the sinking feeling in my gut on the overly plush cushions. I had no idea where this conversation was headed, but it didn't sound good. "Yes, I am."

Her shoulders relaxed. "Then there are a few things you should know that he will be reluctant to tell you." She ran her palms down her pants legs.

Emma voiced encouragement. "Dana, you're doing the right

thing by telling her. She needs to know it all, and you know he won't tell her anyone else's secrets. Not even at the cost of his reputation, or their relationship."

Dana nodded while bracing her palms on her knees. Her spluttered admission stunned me. "My boys are of Clayton's line."

I couldn't hear over the irregular thumping of my heart in my ears. I held my breath to make it slow enough that I could listen again.

Dana's cool hand covered mine briefly. "But they aren't his." She waited a beat and glanced back to Emma. "Or Harper's for that matter."

I gulped air to feed my starving lungs. I'd known they weren't Clayton's, he'd told me as much and I believed him. But Harper—I hadn't been so sure. Not about anything where he was concerned. "Can I ask who their sire is?"

I had seen her boys without glamour. They all shared a very telling birthmark I hadn't known to look for until recently.

"Their father was Marcus Delaney."

"Wow." Talk about your summer/winter romances. I swallowed my surprise. "But you were married to another male."

"I was." Dana studied a plain white-gold band around her finger. "I'm not proud of what I did then, or how I behaved afterwards, but Marcus was a force of nature. Charismatic, handsome, kind, and he loved me."

She twisted the ring. "When I found out I was pregnant, I didn't know what to do. My husband was so happy. His excitement grew almost as fast as my stomach." She wiped a stray tear. "But I loved Marcus and wanted to be with him. We wanted things settled before the boys were born, so I knew I couldn't put it off any longer. We planned to come clean that same night, after they returned from Askara. Only they never came home. My husband died in the same raid we thought had cost you Harper, and so did Marcus."

"I didn't know." I thought back to Clayton's comment about finding Harper as a child in Rihos. "The colonists knew the children weren't your husband's, didn't they?"

"Their wings." She nodded. "They are obviously Delaney's." Her laughter was soft, sorrowful. "I'd wed an Evanti male and was expected to again, just like you. I should have done my job by the colony, but I knew I couldn't go through with it."

"So you used Clayton as your cover." I worked through that line of reasoning. "The crosshatch pattern would match. Everyone would assume you'd had the affair with him and that you were still together instead of pressuring you into a new match."

She nodded, picking at pleats in her pantsuit. "At some point I began to believe my own propaganda, but deep down I knew he had never cared for me that way. I'm ashamed of what I put him through, but using him was easier than owning up to the lies." She glanced up. "After a few months, when I could think beyond getting out of bed each day, I spoke with Emma. She explained about Harper and Clayton." She offered a guilty grin. "It was easier to leave the skeletons in both of our closets. You had protection as Harper's chosen, and I had a few more years of peace."

"Dana, that's enough." We both looked up to find Clayton standing in the den. He could have been a ghost for all the noise made by his approach. A few other males flanked him. They must have overheard our conversation as well. Dana pushed from the couch with flushed cheeks and went back to packing.

Clayton continued forward until he could bend down and

offer me his hand. Pulling me to my feet, he stopped just before kissing me, which did not do at all. I rolled up to my tiptoes and brushed my lips against his, so warm and soft, welcoming.

Emma sighed. "I might as well get this over with." She looked like a child who'd found fuzz on her lollipop. She headed to the staircase. The steady thud of her feet reluctantly climbed higher with every step.

"Are you ready to go?"

Night blacked out the unadorned windows. "I'm not sure how much good I'll be to you in the dark, but I'm game for whatever you have planned."

"Trust me." His mouth found mine again.

It was an easy thing to do. I think some part of me always had.

He addressed the small assembly. "Dillon knows the way to the diner and the movie theatre if any of you feel up to an adventure." A slow smile spread across his lips. "I'll be back sometime tomorrow. Late."

The muscles in my stomach tightened. I think I must have held my breath because the room spun a little. Whatever he saw in my face earned me another kiss and another of those slow smiles.

He led me to the Jeep and helped me inside, then drove past the lights of town until the night swallowed my vision. Without anything to do or see, I rested my head against the back of my seat and closed my eyes, finding the view much the same.

The next thing I knew, I was being shaken awake by a gentle hand on my shoulder. I grumbled, rubbing my eyes as I opened them.

"Sleeping beauty awakens," Clayton teased. "Don't move."

As if I had a choice. The Jeep rocked as his door closed. A moment later he was at my side, opening my door and helping me step out. His arm hung low around my waist, burying beneath my shirt to touch skin as he led me through darkness.

After a moment, I experienced the oddest sensation. Like I'd walked into a spider web and needed to wipe my hands down my arms. The low hum of ambient energy caressed me. "What is that?"

"That is the reason I brought you here tonight." His fingers dug into my hip. "One of the reasons."

I shivered as we walked on and the feeling of power increased. My skin was hyperaware, tingling from the flow of magic across it.

"There's a fallen tree to your left. Just sit. I'll guide you down to it."

I sat, relieved to run my hands over the coarse bark covering of the log. I felt much more at ease with my feet planted firmly on the ground and my bottom settled on the log. It gave me some sense of my surroundings.

"You made it."

I glanced around out of habit and then remembered I couldn't see Figment anyway. "I wondered where you were." Still wondered, actually.

"I've been around, scouting mostly." The sound of her voice was muffled, almost like she was speaking through a tube. *"Magic is a very precise craft, you know."*

"No, I didn't know. I don't have any magic of my own." Nor had I seen anything outside of what glamour could accomplish, so I was curious. "What exactly are you doing?"

"Clayton didn't tell you?"

I heard him off to my right. "I wanted it to be a surprise."

"I don't like surprises." Not when you considered the kind I'd been getting lately.

The log shifted beneath me, bowing under additional weight as he sat down beside me. "You'll like this one."

I leaned over, trying to find him in the dark. "Can I have a hint?"

He captured my searching hand and brought my fingers to his lips to nip across the pads. "Figment is weaving a protective glamour over the new colony site, which is where I've brought you."

I suddenly had a lot more respect for the power held within her quirky body. "That must take a lot of power."

"Yes, it does, which is why she uses hers sparingly." His voice trailed off as a sphere of light danced towards us. The tiny orb stopped and hovered just above my knee.

"I've finished weaving." Sparkles showered my lap. I heard a yawn in her voice. *"This place is larger than the last. I must go to rest. Safe night to you both."*

"Thank you." He lifted the ball, blew gently across it, and sent her drifting away on the slight breeze.

"Bye." I watched her bob in acknowledgement and continue on her way. With her went the light. "So, is that why we came? Seeing Figment without a form was kind of cool, but not exactly worth the drive."

"That's not why we're here." His voice deepened. "Come closer."

Chills spread across my arms, but I did as he asked and scooted until I felt heat rising from his body. "Now what?"

"Come a little closer."

When I shifted to move, he grabbed my waist and tugged me off balance. I braced for impact, still not sure where in this void I was headed, only to come down with an "oomph" and a handful of hard male.

He grunted, but settled me across his lap and tucked my back to his chest. His chin rested on my shoulder as he took my hands and folded them across my lap. "Are you ready?"

I swallowed. "Yes."

He nuzzled my throat, pulling my hair aside to nibble the skin there. "Good, because the show is about to begin."

"What show?"

Almost on cue, a hazy cloud of incandescence extended across the sky, encasing everything in a pale, pulsing light. Tiny sparks rained down around us, sizzling pleasantly as they landed on my skin. Everything touched by Figment's magic twinkled softly.

I looked over my shoulder, finally able to see Clayton in the faint glow. "It's beautiful." I leaned my check against his. "Thanks for sharing this with me."

His answer was a low growl as his hips shifted below me, bringing my attention back to his obvious arousal. I leaned against him, and his heart beat steadily against my back. Lower, he pulsed to the same rhythm, growing larger and firmer beneath me.

"I want you." His hands molded my rib cage, his thumbs teasing the soft undersides of my breasts through the fabric of my shirt. "So much it hurts sometimes."

I rocked my hips across his lap, encouraging him. His hands jerked down to hold me in place. I tried to wiggle, but he held tight. "Did I do something wrong?"

His hands softened. "No." He nipped me where my neck met shoulder. "You're perfect."

"Then why did you stop me?"

"If we do this tonight, I won't let you walk away in the morning." His fingers stroked my side just beneath the hemline of my shirt. "You must be certain of your choice."

Certainty sang through my body. Knowing he was primed for me and feeling his need rise beneath me was more intoxicating than any pheromone.

He slid with me beneath him to the ground. I looked up into his face, backlit by the flickering overhead, and cupped his cheeks between my hands. "I'm sure."

He let me pull him down for another slow meeting of lips, but I needed more. More skin, more of him. My fingers fumbled over the buttons of his shirt, eagerly jerking the shirttail free of his pants and working the shirt from his arms.

I leaned up as far as I was able and rubbed my face across his chest, teasing the flat disk of his male nipple with my tongue. With a slow slide of my nails down his well-muscled chest, I went lower until I found the button of his pants and worked the closure open.

Drawing the zipper down, I slipped my hand beneath the elastic band of his boxers. My fingers tunneled through crisp hairs to find his erection. I stroked him once, twice, glorying in the slide of delicate skin over hard male. When I cupped his sac, the warm weight filled my palm. His body was such a curious mix of textures. I wanted to explore more of him.

"Madelyn." His husky whisper said he wanted me to stop, but the tense lines of his body said otherwise. He captured my seeking hands in his. His shoes were kicked off in the grass, then his pants.

He pulled me upright as he straddled my legs and tugged my shirt overhead. His nimble fingers unhooked my bra and discarded it behind me. All the while, his dark eyes never left mine, sensing perhaps that I needed that connection with him.

When he reached for the closure of my jeans, I lay back down and helped him rid me of the clothing left between us.

He braced over me with one hand planted on the ground just beside my head. His chest lowered to mine and I whimpered at our first touch of naked skin to naked skin. He swallowed the sound, leaving me hungry, desperate to feel his skilled mouth on other parts of my body.

"Tell me I can touch you."

I licked lips gone dry. "Please...touch me."

His dark head lowered, kissing across my collarbone until his eager lips found the tip of my breast and drew it into the moist heat of his mouth. His teeth tugged the hardened peak and I arched up to him, unable to stop my body's reaction. And that wasn't the only one.

Lower, I felt different, wet and soft, ready.

With a final swirl of his tongue, Clayton cupped the small mound in his palm and squeezed. "You can't know how long I've imagined this."

He nuzzled his face between my breasts while his fingers pinched the tips until they pebbled harder against his hands. His lips brushed a trail of light kisses down my stomach towards my navel. When his clever tongue dipped inside, I jerked beneath him.

He continued his downward path with focus that unnerved me. The lower he went, the more I squirmed and scooted to try and keep up with him.

He chuckled softly. "You have to hold still."

"I can't."

"Or won't? Don't you like how this feels?" His sharp teeth closed over my hipbone.

A breathless sigh was all I could manage. I feared the slow

burn building where his kisses neared. Something told me once he reached his destination, he would know exactly how much I enjoyed his ministrations. Heat flashed in my cheeks.

His hands smoothed over and under my hips until he cradled the cheeks of my bottom in his large palms. My legs splayed open, exposing my core to his eager gaze.

"Relax, *deshiel*. I'll stop anytime you tell me to."

My throat closed shut on the protest I knew I should have made. The thought of Clayton as my consort, training my body to respond to his desires, made me quiver in his grasp. Fears of what might have been had I stayed in Askara dissolved beneath his soft lips.

Duty had no place in this. Only desire fueled the string of kisses trailing lower than any male had ever touched. He wanted me, and not the crown or throne or title I no longer bore.

The sudden warm slide of his tongue parting my folds had my elbows digging into earth and my shoulders pushing free of the ground. His fingers gripped tighter as he glanced up and growled like a predator interrupted from his feast.

"I don't think you're supposed to do that."

My breath caught as his face clouded with desire.

"And I'm certain I am." His expression softened just before lowering his head. His tongue entered me again and my legs slapped shut on impulse, locking his face between my thighs. He hummed contentedly, mistaking my uncoordinated reactions for encouragement. Perhaps they were.

He slipped a hand from beneath me to join his mouth in its skilled torture of my tender flesh. He dipped one of his broad fingers inside me, and I gasped and rolled my hips into his palm. My muscles tightened, begged for something more he wouldn't give me. His questing finger stopped just short of some

217

invisible mark.

"Please," I begged. "I need more."

He obliged by inserting a second finger and pumping harder as his tongue laved the pulsing, desperate center of me. One final push and pleasure overcame me. My elbows slipped from beneath me. My back hit the ground as my body shuddered and twitched around his finger and tongue. My trembling legs fell open, and he moved into position between them.

The storm in his blue-gray eyes intensified, blackening seconds before silver swallowed his pupils. His skin darkened, turning the same shade as the night just beyond our cozy bubble of illumination. Then he leaned back to look down at me. "How do you want me?"

"I—" I had no idea how to answer that.

Clayton's glamour fell away as heavy wings arched over me, the thin skin flushing brighter with his intent. His olive-complected skin darkened to a flawless shade of ebony.

For a full second I couldn't breathe. His wings stretched and flexed away from his back. When a shiver moved through him, I answered with a wet rush of moisture where his body met mine. My head turned automatically to allow my eyes to follow every movement of his great, scarlet wings.

"I guess that answers my question."

I hoped it did because my mouth had turned to cotton as his wings twitched and flicked out gracefully behind him. I had to touch one. I reached up, smoothing across the leathery skin. Clayton groaned and their color flared brighter.

I stared. I couldn't help it. With Clayton kneeling between my legs, his wings outstretched and begging for my attention, he was beautiful. I would never forget this night, this claiming. The way his earnest eyes searched mine for assurance or the way his much larger body looked against the night sky still lit by comet-like tails shooting down to earth.

My hands buried in his hair and pulled him down for a kiss. His weight shifted, muscles bunching where his thighs parted my own. He sighed as he thrust against me, rubbing his shaft across my sex.

Hips pushing up to meet him, I drew a strained chuckle from where his cheek pressed against mine. "I need to be inside of you."

Snaking his hand between our bodies, Clayton guided himself to my core. The smooth head of his erection seared me, so much hotter than the rest of his body as it nudged at my entrance. His hips bunched, preparing for entry.

His lips found my ear. "I love you, Maddie. Since that first time I saw you in the gardens of Rihos, I knew you were all there would ever be for me."

His wings snapped out, filling the sky behind him with their ruddy fullness. I couldn't focus when they flittered that way, couldn't help but watch their dance.

The tension thrumming through his body released in that moment of disorientation as he slid deep inside of me, breaking through my virgin barrier.

I gasped as pain and pleasure coalesced, raking his back with my fingernails. "You cheated."

I should have known he would have given such careful thought to this moment. Each gentle rock buried him deeper. My untried muscles strained against his delicious invasion.

His husky chuckle ended on a groan as I wiggled beneath him, trying to get closer and accidentally tensing my inner muscles around him. He rested his forehead on my chest. "I wanted to go slow." He slid out in small degrees then slammed into my core. "I want this to be good for you."

I grabbed his ass and dug in my nails. "Then move."

The thrust and retreat of his body into mine was maddening. He wrapped my legs around his waist, opening me to deeper penetration. And then took it.

His strokes grew harder, longer. His panting breaths matched mine.

"Clayton." I wanted to say the words, needed to give them back to him before this final act joined us together.

His ragged breath caught. "You don't have to say anything." He thrust harder now. My head rolled back. I couldn't think past the pleasure.

The pressure built until I knew something irrevocable was about to happen. I needed to tell him what he meant to me, but it was too late. I cried out his name as my muscles clamped around the hard length of him.

Above me, he growled and surged within me. His back stiffened, muscles straining as his breath rushed out over his lips. Hot spurts filled my shuddering insides as he came.

He dropped his forearms to the ground, resting with our bodies still joined, aligned from head to hip. He brushed sweat-dampened hair from my eyes. He was quiet, and I didn't like it.

The moment was lost and I didn't know how to bring it back. "Clayton—"

He cut me off as his lips brushed my temple. "You're mine. That's enough for now."

But it wasn't enough. Not for me, not for either of us. I couldn't think of anything else to do, so I did the one thing that never failed to get Emma's attention. I pinched him.

He jerked backwards, as startled by my attack as I was. "What was that for?"

"For being so damn accepting of me, for being willing to

settle when you deserve better. You told me you loved me—"

"And I do."

"Then you will shut up and hold still long enough to let me tell you that I love you too."

He blinked, still rubbing the sore spot. Then dimples pierced his cheeks. "Can I hear it again?"

"I love you, Clayton Delaney, and you're stuck with me now because I claim you as my male, as is my right."

His lips curved upward before they covered mine. The fading lightshow flickered out to leave us in darkness. As the last glimmer left the sky, I pulled his chest back down to mine, feeling him stir within me as I breathed in the scent of male and sex.

My male, and the first of many times I planned to lay claim to him tonight.

About the Author

Hailey Edwards lives in a fantasyland of her own creation, where her closest neighbors are Cairine House vampires, Bay Cerise werewolves, and a colony full of Evanti demons.

To explore Hailey's world, visit her website at www.HaileyEdwards.net, or to find out all of her latest news, check her blog, www.CairineHouse.com.